THE AUTHENTIC LEADER AS SERVANT (ALS)

ALS I COURSE 3
EMULATION LEADERSHIP
Attributes, Principles, and Practices

SYLVANUS N. WOSU, Ph.D

THE AUTHENTIC LEADER AS SERVANT
ALS I COURSE 3
Emulation Leadership Attributes, Principles, and Practices

© Copyright 2024 by Sylvanus N. Wosu Ph.D.

Printed in the United States of America
ISBN: 978-8-9866440-3-5

All rights reserved. No part of this book may be reproduced or transmitted in any form or by any means, electronic or mechanical, including photocopying, recording, or by any information storage and retrieval system, without permission in writing from the copyright owner.

Bible quotations are from the New King James (NKJV) version of the Bible unless otherwise indicated.

Other versions used in this book are the New International Version (NIV), New Living Translation (NLT), King James Version (KJV), English Standard Version (ESV), and Good News Translation (GNT). Unless otherwise specified, NKJV should be assumed.

The views expressed in this work are solely those of the author and do not necessarily reflect the views of the publisher, and the publisher disclaims any responsibility for them.

To order additional copies of this book, contact:
Proisle Publishing Services LLC
39-67 58th Street, 1st floor
Woodside, NY 11377, USA
Phone: (+1 646-480-0129)
info@proislepublishing.com

Table of Contents

FOREWORD — XI
ACKNOWLEDGMENTS — XV
DEDICATION — XVII
PREFACE — 19
   About Leader As Servant Leadership (LSL) Model — 22
   About the Authentic Leader as Servant (ALS) — 25
   About the ALS Courses — 26

CHAPTER 1
UNDERSTANDING LEADERSHIP ATTRIBUTES — 35
   Functional Definitions — 35
   Comparisons With Other Works — 40
   Principle of Leadership Attribute — 42
   Authentic Leadership Attributes — 43
   Summary 1 Understanding Leadership Process — 49

CHAPTER 2
LEADERSHIP EMULATION ATTRIBUTE — 53
   Characteristics of Emulation Attribute — 53
   Principle of Emulation Attribute — 55
   Summary 2 Leadership Emulation Attribute — 57

CHAPTER 3
DEVELOPING THE ACTS OF EMULATION-INSPIRATION — 61
   Inspiration by a Desire to Imitate Christ — 61
   Summary 3 Developing the Acts of Emulation-Inspiration — 63

CHAPTER 4
DEVELOPING THE ACTS OF EMULATION-INITIATION — 65
   initiate a desire to emulate your own will — 65
   Seven Patterns for Good works: — 67
   Summary 4 Developing the Acts of Emulation-Initiation — 68

CHAPTER 5
DEVELOPING THE ACTS OF EMULATION-MODELING — 71
   Strategies to Model Emulation — 72
   Modeling temperance through self-control — 76
   Summary 5 Developing the Acts of Attentive Discipleship — 77

CHAPTER 6
DEVELOPING THE ACTS OF REPRODUCTIVE DISCIPLESHIP 79
Following the example and leave no alternative option. -------- 79
Following the Christ-like image to emulate ------------------- 80
Following Your Priorities with Passion ---------------------- 81
Summary 6 Developing the Acts of Reproductive Discipleship -------- 84

TOPIC INDEX   89
REFERENCES   91

FOREWORD

The modern world today is obsessed with standardization and modalities. As a result, in the realm of leadership, many books have spout associated leadership theories and models and explain them as the path to follow. However, the critical dimensions that distinguish the effectiveness of any leadership process are the values and attribute the leader brings to the table; desired change is influenced by leadership styles or standards. These many standards and theories of leadership often are not in step with the changing times or the followers' needs. The trend is a bit like stocking different kinds of foods in a grocery store and expecting that they will meet everybody's needs the same way and at all times. Aisles are packed with varieties of food with expiration dates in the future, but getting the best deal on the products is what really matters to those who buy and use the products

In many ways, this is the state of leadership in the modern world. Increasingly, even leaders of public institutions are tasked with turning a profit for themselves or the organization they serve. The idea of a "leader" seems to float uneasily alongside the ranks of fundraisers or profit raisers in contrast to any kind of role model for followers or employees. That which is knowable, measurable, and marketable has surpassed the difficult intangibility of strong moral leadership attributes as the central guideline for achievement and success.

In this complicated space, Dr. Sylvanus Wosu introduces his complex idea of the Leader as a Servant Leadership, which is in this book, modeled on Christian tradition. Like all intricate ideas, Dr. Wosu's central point depends on a paradox: a person is best qualified to lead when he or she is most ready to serve. This paradox has been monopolized rhetorically by "public servants" who often serve either self-interest or the interests of specific lobbies. The Authentic Leader as Servant penetrates past the superficial concept of "serving" and details the internal state of true servitude or Servanthood.

While the book is primarily focused on the Christian model of leadership attributes such as discipleship, empathy, affection, and Servanthood, it does so not merely on the grounds of blind faith, but rather via numerous contemporary sociological and business-driven studies on how leaders should seek a leader-follower relationship that is simultaneously productive and nurturing. Dr. Wosu's most piercing insights always involve this secular–Christian dialogue. This book demonstrates that Christ's model for leadership is one that may exist successfully outside the confines of a faith relationship; it places the values of Christ's religious significance in leadership at the center of the framework. It is clear from Dr. Wosu's generous own life story of faith—a faith tested by humbling difficulties—is at the center of both his orientation and motivation for writing.

In language that is so concise, it is often illustrated in mathematical formulas; Dr. Wosu explains the deep structural integrity of Christ's Leader as the Servant Leadership model. One could imagine leaders of any doctrine benefiting from the analyses contained in these pages. The book's message repeatedly encourages the reader to imagine a scenario or reflect on memories and personal experiences to prove or test its many points. Thus, the book depends on a form of praxis, a lesson that could be or has been enacted, by the participating reader. I am very impressed at the volume and level of thinking of the author. Parts of the book involve his personal story, which is especially riveting. I cannot imagine what he had to endure, which he referred to as a" wilderness walk," to accomplish the goal he set for himself. His life stories on these pages are inspiring and stimulating.

In this way, the text eschews dogmatism in favor of the self-discovery Socratic Method of teaching and learning. The reader is not badgered into complying with a religious objective but is rather asked to consider the applicability of difficult biblical concepts in relation to modern life. It is a fascinating and very thought-provoking read.

Hence, the book does not seek to make the leader a servant, a cookie-cutter corporate buzzword, but rather asks the reader to imagine him or herself interacting with a range of concepts. One of Dr. Wosu's great strengths is his reservation when it comes to forcing his reading's interpretation on the material he presents.

The book parallels Biblical and modern leadership scenarios in ways that consistently provoke thought, and while it is clear Dr. Wosu has his particular leadership style; the space for the reader's own thoughts is always left open.

Foreword

The book could not have been written in any other way with integrity. Its format and formulas are offered to the reader of the leader as a servant role that it analyzes in its pages. To find a text that instructs from this humble position is profoundly refreshing in a genre that is often packaged inside a cover with a sizeable picture of the "modest" author, smiling egotistically beneath a name spelled out in large, gold lettering. Throughout its pages, this text feels as if it serves the reader.

In the end, this is the most satisfying aspect of the book. There is no standardized approach to achieving successful leadership. There is no promise of power and a bigger payday; in fact, the book often proffers just the opposite. The reader is not encouraged to devalue the experience of leadership by finding some economic metric for marking success but is rather asked to think deeply about the most basic elements of internal and social interaction within the framework of a Christian tradition. What this means will be different for every reader. Indeed, even in the context of single chapters, I found myself questioning or re-evaluating moments of my own life. This book serves; it doesn't feel like filling in multiple-choice questions, staring at a wall of flavorless grocery products, or hearing the endless servant promises of today's political scene. It feels like a humble invitation to consider a single paradoxical element of a profoundly productive tradition.

-Tobias Bates

Acknowledgments

A book on leadership attributes as aspects of Servant Leadership sprouted from the wealth of knowledge and the inspirations of many other leaders. Their writings were sources of inspiration, challenges, and examples of excellence to emulate.

Dr. Enefaa N. Wosu, my wife and life partner, for her love, commitment, and prayer support, especially during those long night hours I was not there for her and her constant reminder of who I must be as a leader-servant. Without her support, forbearance, wisdom, and encouragement, this project would not have been completed; I say, thank you very much.

And to God alone be all the glory and honor for the divine inspiration and guidance in initiating and completing this life-transforming book project.

DEDICATION

I humbly submit this book back unto the gracious hands of God who inspired the writings through His Holy Spirit!

I dedicate this book to my virtuous wife of 45 years, Rev. (Dr.) Enefaa Wosu whose spiritual leadership is an important gateway to our home, and to our four wonderful children—Prof. Eliada Wosu-Griffin EL, HeCareth, Tamuno-Emi, and Chidinma. From them all, I learnt what it meant to be a leader-servant. I could not be blessed with better teachers.

PREFACE

What characteristics did Biblical leaders like the Apostle Paul, Moses, Joshua, and Nehemiah as servants of their people display outwardly that distinguished them from other leaders, both then and now? The Apostle Paul kept his focus to *emulate* Christ and endured all the infirmities and persecutions he suffered to complete his goal to preach the gospel of Jesus Christ. He inspired Timothy and others through his effective *discipleship* leadership to imitate him as he emulated Christ. Moses' outward display of his *trust* in God's power earned him a good level of trust from the people and empowered him for the mission of delivery of God's children from bondage in Egypt; he had to *reproduce* himself in Joshua to complete the mission. But the greatest of them was Jesus Christ, who humbly sacrificed His life to finish the work of redemption. In His *Servanthood*, commitment, and love for the people, He became the ultimate *model* of a leader as a servant to *emulate*.

Let's consider for a moment secular leaders in these current times! For example, think of Henry Ford, who founded the successful Ford Motor Company; Bill Gates who created the global empire that is Microsoft; Albert Einstein, who in many ways is synonymous with a genius for his contributions to modern physics; Abraham Lincoln, remembered as one of the greatest presidents and leaders of United States; and many others like these we cannot mention. What did all these leaders have in common? What propelled them to turn their initial failures or challenges into eventual successes? None had a direct mentor or inherited any fortune from their parents. Nevertheless, they all eventually succeeded. These people can be distinguished from others based on their self-will to succeed, their self-confidence and belief in themselves, their self-determination, and their perseverance, among other characteristics. The distinguishing characteristics displayed externally in service or relationships toward others are the outward functional attributes that define that leader.

Think about yourself as a student, faculty member, or that new executive. What was it that made your journey to success different and even great? Students and colleagues, when they see or hear about my display of what I have referred to as the 'wilderness walk of faith', have asked me to share the critical attitudinal elements that made me remain inwardly resilient and undaunted and yet outwardly joyful in the difficulties I had faced. This book is the result of those reflections. Let me explain one such teaching moment.

Many years ago, sitting in my research lab on a Saturday morning trying to finish writing my dissertation, a fellow graduate student walked into the room to talk with me. He was contemplating terminating his graduate studies. He was a privileged single male student but felt the load was just too much.

"Sylvanus," he asked, with seriousness in his eyes, "your research advisor suggested that I should ask you, 'what is it that makes you tick?'.'What is it about you that makes you joyful and at peace with yourself and determined to finish, no matter the situations and high expectations we face in this department?"

What he asked me were deeply reflective questions, but I was willing and excited to answer them. Even so, before I do, let's look at the context. At that period in my life, I had four little children as a graduate student; in fact, more children than any of the faculties at that time, except for one faculty member who had eight children. I received little or no support from the department. I was then an international alien, did not qualify for financial aid, and was not given any research assistant position. I was, therefore, self-supported with two off-campus part-time jobs. I joked at being a minority of minorities, the only student in the department with such a label,—but I was self-willed to succeed. My adaptability attribute, coupled with perseverance and resilience, was all that I needed to succeed despite the odds against me. In every exam, homework assignment, or project I had to compete with students with full financial aid, plus they had nothing to distract their attention from their studies. I lived with the attitude that using disadvantages as an excuse was not an option. Aspiring to earn my Ph.D. was a life dream, and I was willing to give my ultimate best to actualize that dream even in the face of challenges. The choice was mine!

So I looked at my classmate and all I could see was a student striding through a valley through which I also walked. He needed me to show him how to walk the walk, to empathize with him. To answer his question, I smiled, not that I wanted to, but because it was just who

I was. The joy he attributed to me was an overflow of my appreciation of God's grace that His life in me was externally manifesting His light to bless someone else. It was a great teaching moment; I capitalized on it to tell my classmate that my joy was not about me. He could see physically but about He who was in me, he could not see in the flesh; I needed him to know that I was just showing forth His life in me. At first, my classmate did not understand the spiritual prose or metaphor I was using. He looked surprised but open to hearing more.

I did not ask if he was a Christian. However, right on my desk was my small green pocket Bible. I opened to 2 Corinthians 12:9 (NIV) and handed it to him to read. As he read the passage: "But he said to me, 'My grace is sufficient for you, for my power is made perfect in weakness.' Therefore, I will boast all the more gladly about my weaknesses, so that Christ's power may rest on me," I noticed how absorbed he was in the words

He looked astonished and read it again, this time silently. "This is interesting, but what does this mean?" He asked. I took his question to mean, "How does this relate to my question?

I explained to my friend that the external attitudes he or my advisors saw in me that warranted the question, "What makes you tick" were inspired by my inner value system based on my faith in this same Christ and His teachings. My desire to manifest His life and self-confidence is all because of what He has promised in His word if I believed. I have believed His words and have gained self-determination and faith to make the right choices through Him for my life, and his spirit has given me perseverance and resilience to focus on finishing strong in pursuit of any goal. "With that faith, I have continued, more passionately and excitedly; I can look at my challenges and vulnerabilities and delight joyfully in them, even as an alien minority of minorities! His grace and power have empowered me to do all things I want to do. That is what makes me tick," I explained.

He looked at me as if he got his answer. "Wow, thanks!" he said, looking inspired and ready to face his challenges. As we concluded with a prayer, and he stood up to leave, I pointed empathetically to his face and said, "If I made it despite my challenges, you have absolutely no excuse but to persevere to complete your studies; you can make it too!"

It is fitting to report that this encounter with my classmate transformed his will and determination to continue. Yes, he was encouraged and went on to complete his graduate studies. He emulated self-will and perseverance from the example of the most vulnerable of all students in the department.

The inner value system of a Leader-Servant is founded not only on his faith but his self-will, coupled with self-leadership; it is the greatest mentor who can turn any situation into an inconceivable success. Self-will is the primary driver for determination, resilience, and perseverance. It is what wakes you up in the morning to ask for strength to do whatever it is you are setting out to do. Based on my life walk of faith, I can state with absolute certainty that faith is the unseen assuredness that can empower you to turn your life's probable impossibilities into great and improbable possibilities.

ABOUT LEADER AS SERVANT LEADERSHIP (LSL) MODEL

Looking at the testimony above, do you know the source that energizes the characteristics you display outside and how your inner self is related to what others see outside? What distinguishes you from others is what combines to define your attributes! As a follower, can you identify the characteristics that distinguish your leaders? As an executive, how do you base your evaluation of yourself? Or how do you evaluate that brand-new manager or new youth director you want to hire? To what do you compare the individual's qualities when you look at his CV? What is the basis of your measure? Do you know if you are a substantial leader? These personal questions and much more are the subjects of this two-volume book, 'The Authentic Leader as Servant Part I: The Outward Leadership Attributes, Principles, and Practices', is written in two parts; the second part 'The Leader as Servant Leadership Model. Part II'; deals with the Inner Strength Leadership Attributes, Principles, and Practices.

When we think about today's corporate greed, deepening divide between the haves and have-not, gridlock in political systems, conflicts and wars, high divorce rates, and the rich young ruler in the Bible, it is easy to agree that all these people share a few things in common: self-centeredness, pride, lack of compassion, and greed. There is a great need in today's suffering world for leader-servants who display leadership attributes. These attributes should be oriented toward selfless service to others. Indeed, our world is increasingly drifting away from global serving reality toward the self and apathy. The most credible message or model for a possible solution to this dilemma and the answer to several complex leadership questions can be found in the foundation of the ultimate leader-servant, Jesus Christ. This book defines the Leader as Servant Leadership attribute as the combined acts of two or more distinctive functional leadership characteristics exhibited in service and relationship toward others. There is no better time than now for a book that presents comprehensive and irrevocable facts and principles regarding how to develop effective attributes of the leader-servant.

The Leader as Servant Leadership Model

My first book on this subject, The Leader as Servant Leadership Model, explains that Jesus' servant leadership model is based on the notion of a Leader as a Servant and not on a Servant as Leader. There are four distinct differences between a Servant as Leader (Servant-leader) and the Leader as Servant (leader--servant) models. It is pertinent to highlight them here to connect to this book, Authentic Leader as Servant.

A Leader as Servant is a leader first. The leader–servant as a leader does not in the line of duty go projecting or lording his or her power and authority over others but is the person to lead the process of influencing desired changes in others through his humble example of being a servant or having a serviceable attitude toward others. He or she is a serving leader, not a lording leader. He leads as a servant by putting others' needs above his own needs and rights. Jesus emphasized the word "as" meaning that the leader (the Master) chooses to serve as a servant even though he is the leader. A leader–servant emulates Jesus, who gave up all rights, and emptied and expended Himself on His followers. He empowered them to become more like Him. A leader-servant is known as a leader first but is seen as a great leader by his humble attendant heart and acts of service to others. His greatness comes from his ability to put others above himself.

Leader as Servant is a Biblical Concept. The model or image of a humble serving leader motivated Jesus' disciples to see that if their master could do this for them, they must also be able to do it for others. Jesus clearly demonstrated the process of leader-as-servant leadership. In some cases, He chose to serve by leading when He wanted to create the image or model of the leader-servant in certain acts. In other cases, He chose to lead by serving, when he showed care and empathy toward the people and led the disciples to see empathy as a leadership attribute.

Leader as Servant is an Authentic Leadership Model to follow. The Leader as the Servant leadership model intentionally positions Jesus as an original model of a leader to follow.

He was serving His disciples to demonstrate that the process of becoming a great leader was earned through humble acts of service to others; He made them understand that He was empowering them to succeed Him as leader-servants through service to others. The result was an incomparable legacy of leadership that changed their communities. The fact that Jesus relinquished his rights or shared His power did not diminish His power and influence. In fact, his influence increased at least 11 X 100%, if we ignore the one case of Judas.

The Leader as Servant Transforms Organizational Culture. The proposed LSL model seeks to transform and sustain the community or organization by instilling key leadership values or "leadership presence" among followers or an organization's members. Change is sustained when everyone in the organization takes ownership of the change. Rather than focusing on leading more followers to be great followers who conform to the organizational culture, LSL seeks to lead and empower better leaders to be distinguished leaders and community builders.

There are four distinctions, which clearly differentiate many of the existing servants as Leader-based philosophies in relation to servant leadership from my LSL model. Even in the corporate or institutional worlds, there is nothing better than Jesus on which to base Servant Leadership. There is nothing more authentic and impacting than the servant leadership modeled by the life and teachings of Jesus Christ.

The LSL model uses exploratory questions, scenarios, and graphic visualizations to excite critical thinking in ways no other book on this subject has yet attempted. Several personal testimonies of my wilderness walk of faith with God are used to connect the reader to real-life experiences of the concepts discussed. The riveting effect is that the text engages and encourages the reader to walk through the experiences presented. The aim is to inspire the reader spiritually, mentally, and professionally with this far-reaching exposition on the subject of servant leadership.

ABOUT THE AUTHENTIC LEADER AS SERVANT (ALS)

The *Authentic Leader as Servant* argues that no leadership model is as authentic, other-centered, able to build communities, and productive and service-oriented as the model of our ultimate leader-servant, Jesus Christ. No source can provide a better point of reference than that provided in the Bible. Hence, this book aims to be more than just a text on leadership; it hopes to be a personal discovery for those who aspire to develop effective leadership attributes that grow leaders as servants who ultimately develop thriving other-centered communities. This book presents a comprehensive, biblically-based study regarding how to develop these attributes and how they are applied in a servant leadership process. In this biblical context and for clarity, Servant Leadership means *Leader-as-Servant Leadership*. A *leader-servant* refers to a *leader as a servant*, which is distinct from a servant-leader or servant as leader.

Leader as Servant Leadership attributes are shaped by the Leadership's Inner Value system, which consists of character, motivation, and commitment. The *Authentic Leader as Servant* is presented as a necessary resource to complement my *The Leader as Servant Leadership (LSL) Model*. The LSL model integrates a transformative leadership framework and interactive dimensions of Servant Leadership. Leader as Servant Leadership is a process in which a leader, in his leadership position, purposefully chooses to put others' rights and needs above his positional rights and personal needs. He then serves, enables, and empowers followers for growth that builds a thriving organization. The LSL model looks at the predominant Servant Leadership concepts and shares how they compare with biblical principles on how we should lead and be led.

ABOUT THE ALS COURSES

The three books, *LSL Model* and *The Authentic Leader as Servant (*Parts I and II), together demonstrate that with today's global visions to reach people of all races and cultures, now is the time for an authentic servant's heart of service. Those visions and the leadership processes are most effective with the appropriate leadership attributes centered more on people than on the organization, principles regarding how to develop effective attributes of leader-servant.

The ALS I and II combined presented twenty leaders as servant leadership attributes. The series of ALS courses supply training guide to understand, develop, and practice the attributes in a leadership process. Each course is independent and self-contained and does not depend on completing any other course in the series of 20 courses. It is, however strongly recommended, in fact a must read, that chapters 1 and 2 in each series be covered as they lay the foundation of LSL model on which ALS is based.

ALS (Parts I & II) Course Layout

The *Authentic Leader as Servant (ALS)* leadership (parts I and II) book has been broken down into 20 courses in workbook format to achieve three goals 1) Self-discovery of the acts of developing the attribute under review in the course, 2) deeper understanding of the principles, research and biblical teaching behind the attributes, and 3) Learning the strategies for practicing the attributes.

Instruction

The set of questions following each chapter are designed to serve as a guide to discover, explore, and practice the essential ALS leadership attributes, principles, and practices in leadership process. The questions are comprehensive review based on the content of this specific chapter only.

To maximize the learning outcomes, the learner must read through this chapter and sections. Some referenced scriptures in the book are repeated in the summaries for added review if needed, even though they were discussed in the section in which they apply.

> The exercises that follow each chapter will help you in not only understanding your own strength and weaknesses in your acts of the attribute but will guide you in developing practical strategies you can apply in self-leadership process or helping others grow in leadership
>
> All answers to the questions are contained in the associated chapter or sections; consultation of new sources, except for the reference scriptures, is not needed. Thus, it is expected that you answer the questions after you have read the associated section or chapter of the workbook. The scripture or other references cited are only for references as they already discussed in the book

ALS I Course 1: Affection Leadership Attribute—*Affection flows from a person to produce positive emotions for the well-being of another person.*

An average person will define the word "love" in the sense that affection is a characteristic of love. Nevertheless, that definition clouds the functional meaning of affection as an attribute of a leader-servant. Affection is a love action intentionally given to someone to create favorable emotion. We experience a positive emotion when we receive or give affection. In his acts of affection, the Apostle Paul communicated to the Corinthian Christians how he spoke to them freely with an open heart, because it was an important way to give affection (2 Corinthians 6:11-13). He also spoke of longing for them with the affection of Jesus Christ (Philippians 1:8); an affection that needs to be mutual (1 Peter 1:7). How is the affection leadership attribute an outward leadership attribute? This course explores this and other questions to discover the characteristics of affection attributes and to formulate a functional principle based on the expected outcome of affection and the effective use of these attributes in leadership.

ALS I Course 2: Discipleship Leadership Attribute- *Discipleship transforms and empowers followers for service leadership that grows communities.*

Discipleship as an act of developing a follower toward a specific goal is an important function of leadership to equip others to lead. *Discipleship transforms and empowers followers for service leadership that grows communities*. A disciple is a follower who willingly chooses to follow the master and submits to his discipleship and authority. In that regard, Jesus wanted all his followers to be his disciples and ambassadors because a disciple is always a follower. Organizationally, a follower could be a junior employee, any employee in a brand-new department, a new younger faculty, or just any person that needs to be guided through a journey of professional growth and good success. This course focuses on the general growth of followers through the acts of discipleship and presents the critical characteristics of discipleship as a leadership outward attribute. Functional definitions of leadership discipleship attributes and its principle will be presented based on those characteristics. Each characteristic will be discussed in detail with emphasis on strategies of how they can be further developed or practiced as a part of the servant leadership process.

ALS I Course 3: Emulation Leadership Attribute—*A great leader-servant outwardly and positively inspires a pattern of good works for others to follow.*

To emulate is to strive to be like someone else or to follow someone else's example by imitating something that inspires you about that person. This course evaluates how to learn from someone good leadership qualities to develop yours. How did you use what you learned from following the footstep of your hero to grow your leadership qualities. Jesus in the scripture modeled humility and Servanthood he wanted his disciples to develop same qualities. Emulation as a leadership attribute shares some characteristics with transformative leadership, where a leader intentionally conveys a clear vision of a goal, inspires the passion for the work toward the goal, and motivates the followers to follow. As a leader, how do you model a characteristic behavior for someone to follow or develop? How is Leadership Emulation Leadership Attribute an outward leadership attribute? This course explores this and other questions to discover the characteristics of affection attributes and to formulate a functional principle based on the expected outcome of effective use of these attributes in leadership.

ALS I Course 4: Generosity Leadership Attribute: *Generosity is an outward measure of the level of sacrifice, what is shared, or the impact a giving makes, not just the size of the giving*

Generosity can be defined as "the *habit of giving* without expecting anything in return. It can involve offering time, assets, or talents to aid someone in need." Such habits can include spending your personal money, time, and/or labor for the welfare of others or expending (suffering or being consumed or spending) for others' well-being. When political leaders or Board members 'vote their conscience' on important issues that affect others, what is that "conscience" and how do such leaders contribute to the welfare of others? How can you, "Do all you can, with what you have, in the time you have, in the place where you are" for the betterment of humanity All giving to help humanity is crucial to help meet the needs of the most vulnerable of God's children, as demonstrated by God as attribute of God, In this course, we will explore what distinguishes a leader's act of giving from his inside intentions. The key leadership characteristics of generosity will be discussed with respect to Servant-Leadership generosity Attributes and Principles and the details how a leader-servant can develop those characteristics and then effectively practice service leadership.

ALS I Course 5: Healing-Care Leadership Attribute: *Comforting others in any trouble with the comfort with which God comforts us, brings healing-wholeness*

What is healing Care and what does it mean in practical terms to you as a leader? Effective leadership begins with an emotionally and spiritually healthy leader who can reconcile and bring comfort to the followers, irrespective of followers' feelings (good or bad) toward the leader. The healing attribute and personal security complement each other. You must have the capacity for self-healing and individual security if you are to meet others' comforts. Personal security provides the infrastructure to support leaders in adversity and heal others that are hurting. A leader's or a group's success is measured by the strength of the weakest member or follower in the group or team… Healing is one of the most abstract and least understood attributes in leadership, and yet one of the most important. The key distinguishing characteristics will be explored to formulate a working definition and principle of leadership healing-care attributes based on those characteristics. Each characteristic will be discussed in detail with emphasis on strategies of how they can be further developed or practiced by a leader-servant as part of the servant leadership process.

ALS I Course 6: Influence Leadership Attribute-*The true measure of leadership success in affecting desired change in conduct, performance, and relational connections in others is influence*

Leadership is an integrative process in which a person applies appropriate (leadership) attributes to guide and influence the desired attitudinal changes in others toward accomplishing a particular goal. Eight five percent of CEOs of top companies surveyed on their climb to leadership ladder said they were "influenced by another leader," compared to 10% and 5% for "natural gifting" and "result of a crisis," respectively. When we consider influence as a servant leadership attribute, we are talking about a distinguishing leadership characteristic that displays on the outside what a leader is inside, influence takes on a deeper meaning. In this course, the key leadership characteristics of influence will be identified and explored from research to frame definitions of the Servant-Leadership influence attribute and principle. Based on those characteristics, the key outcomes of effective leadership influence l how a leader-servant can develop those characteristics and then effectively practice service leadership.

ALS I Course 7: Persuasion Leadership Attribute—*The means of transforming others to a new perspective is through empathetic persuasion.*

Persuasion attribute affords the leader the capacity to convince his followers or others to believe and engage in a new idea or goal through encouragement rather than using his positional authority or intimidation. Because members of the group may already have their views on an issue, the leader must carefully approach persuasion as a learning process to avoid conflicts or polarizing the group. He must unify the diversity of views to get buy-in and willingness to agree and follow. The leader-servant primarily relies on making decisions within an organization based on persuasion rather than positional authority. In other words, you will never hear the Leader-servant say, "Do it because I am the boss, and I say to." This particular element offers one of the clearest distinctions between the traditional authoritarian model of leadership and the concept of Servant leadership. In this course, we will explore the technique of convincing rather than coercing as one of the most effective ways a leader-servant can build consensus within groups. Key characteristics of persuasion leadership attribute will be found, fully discussed, and modeled from the examples in the lives of other leaders.

ALS I Course 8: Reproduction Leadership Attribute—*Great leaders produce successors for legacy and greater courses as an expected product of an effective leadership reproduction.*

In his book, *360 Degree Leader*, John C. Maxwell says, "Great leaders don't use people so they can win. They lead people so they can all lead together." Such great leaders, like Jesus, Moses, Paul, and others developed other leaders through a process of reproduction. Is it possible for leaders of today to reproduce their vision in others so that can lead and build a legacy together? The answer to this question is of course yes. However, the effectiveness of a leader duplicating his leadership qualities in a follower depends on the leadership reproduction attribute of the leader. This course explores the distinguishing characteristics of reproduction as an outward attribute in servant leadership. Functional definitions of leadership reproduction attribute and its principle will be presented based on those characteristics. Each characteristic of reproduction attributes will be discussed in detail with emphasis on strategies of how they can be further developed or practiced by a leader-servant as part of the servant leadership process.

ALS I Course 9: Servanthood Leadership Attribute— *A leader-servant is most qualified to lead when ready to serve as a servant for the growth of others.*

The last time you engaged in a practical act of service on the job, at home, church, or in your community, what were the key elements in that act of service? Did you serve because you wanted to and chose to serve? Or was it because someone asked you to? The ultimate goal is for the leader's life to positively transform many lives in his or her community of followers. Consider the New Testament teachings of Jesus, who demonstrated the ultimate Leader as Servant Leadership. Jesus equated greatness to serving unpretentiously (humbly, as would a child), and He equated leading with choosing to serve others. That is the first affirmative test of authenticity for this attribute. What were the distinguishing characteristics that enabled you to serve? How is the Leadership Servanthood an outward leadership attribute? This course will give answers and meanings to these and personal reflective questions to discover the distinguishing characteristics of The Leadership Servanthood attribute. Functional definitions of The Leadership Servanthood attribute and principle will be provided based on the identified characteristics. Readers will benefit from numerous techniques, personal examples, empirical case study, and applications of the concepts.

ALS I Course 10: Trust-Integrity Leadership Attribute—*True leadership trust produces assured trustee's confidence and readiness to follow based on the credibility, competence, and shared relational connections of the trusted.*

A study examined more than 75 key components of employee satisfaction in top leadership and found that trust and confidence was the single most reliable predictor of employee satisfaction in an organization. This course will examine the results of the above study with respect to servant leadership, and how a leader-servant increases the satisfaction of the followers in an organization. When the organization is going through some challenges, how can a leader be credible in helping the followers understand the company's mission and strategy? How can he share information on how the company or institution, or department is doing and how the followers or employees will be affected? Suppose the organization's strategy is not aligned with its inner value or character, how does the leader build trust in followers or earn trust from them? Organizational leadership trust has been defined by as "an employee's willingness to take a risk for a leader with the expectation that, in exchange, the leader will behave in some desired way." The course will examine how the element of reliance and confidence in the actions of the trusted and organization are characterized by a combination of Competence (Can they do the job?), Benevolence (Do they care about me?), and Integrity (Are they honest?).

Referenced Scriptures

A variety of Bible translations from over 11,200 original Hebrew, Aramaic, and Greek words to about 6,000 English words do exist with variations in meanings and emphases. I am not a biblical scholar and do not pretend to be one; Hence, I have avoided researching the roots of these words and personally prefer New King James Version (NKJV). I have intentionally used other translations for three main reasons; first, to allow for increased impact and alignment of words to the most desired meaning and emphasis in the concepts being addressed. Second, I wanted new and personal discovery of meanings from translations with which I have not been familiar. And third, I wanted to allow readers who may desire translations other than the NKJV the benefit of their preferred translations. Hence, in addition to the NKJV, other translations used in the book include New International Version (NIV), New Living Translation (NLT), King James Version (KJV), English Standard Version (ESV), and Good News Translation (GNT). Unless otherwise specified, NKJV should be assumed.

Sylvanus Nwakanma Wosu

CHAPTER 1
UNDERSTANDING LEADERSHIP ATTRIBUTES

Leadership attribute is the combined acts of two or more distinctive functional leadership characteristics exhibited in service and relationship toward others.

The starting point of our discussion is the understanding of the key functional definitions and concepts that describe the theme of this book. In general, 1 will define leadership as an integrative process in which a person applies appropriate attributes to guide and influence the sought-after attitudinal changes in others toward accomplishing a particular goal. Specifically, the Leader as Servant Leadership is a process in which a leader intentionally chooses to put the follower's rights and needs above his positional rights and personal needs, and serves, enables, and empowers them for desired spiritual and professional growth that builds thriving communities.

FUNCTIONAL DEFINITIONS

In the context of these definitions, I will begin the descriptions of the leadership attributes of an authentic leader-servant by offering a functional definition of Leadership Attributes, and showing how that definition differs from those of Leadership Character, Characteristics, and Traits.

Leadership Character is the sum total of personal qualities in leadership, such as honesty, values, vision, trust, and so on that make up the moral capital of the leader; Leadership character should describe who the leader is inside or the leader's basic personality traits.

The Leadership Characteristics describe the distinctive characteristics or features of a leader, such as attitudes, competencies, skills, and specific experiences that go beyond his character (personality). Leadership characteristics determine how (through skills and competencies) the leader leads or take actions in the process of leadership in any particular situation;

The Leadership traits are the distinguishing leadership characteristics of a leader (these are things that define his leadership characteristics), which differentiate from personality traits... Leadership traits are the set of characteristics that define a particular leader's leadership. This means that a leadership characteristic is a trait when it is a unique characteristic of the leader.

Leadership Attributes, unlike leadership character, characteristics, and traits, is *a leadership attribute and the combined act of two or more distinctive functional leadership characteristics exhibited in service and relationship toward others* or traits externally displayed in action toward others. All leadership attributes grow out of the leadership inner value system but can be externally displayed predominantly as an outbound or outward attribute or both:

1. **Outbound Attributes:** These are distinctive outward-bound attributes emanating from the inner strength of the leader to support external conduct in service and relationships toward others. They form the internal core functional qualities that motivate or enhance the outward manifestation of the inside character toward others. The outbound attribute such as listening and vision, for example, are the direct results of the inner values of the leader such as patience, hearing, love, humility, or all the fruits of the spirit.

2. **Outward Attributes:** These are distinctive functional outward outer visible attributes emanating from the richness of the outbound and inner values of the leader. For example, external attributes such as Servanthood, emulation/modeling, empathy, etc. are outflows from the leader who will directly impact the follower. Outward attributes can be enriched by the outbound (inner) attributes. As shown in

Figure 1, the outward attributes in general form the outer core of functional attributes in the leader as servant leadership, but they can share some overlapping functions with the outbound attributes.

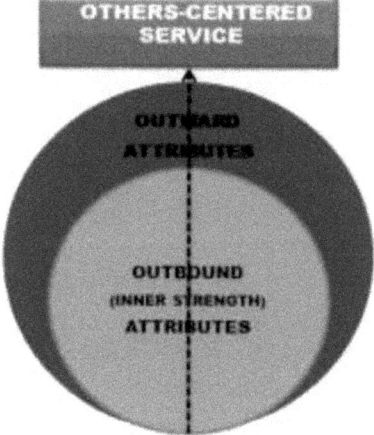

Figure 1.1. Servant leadership functional attributes

In summary, a leadership attribute is more than an ability or a characteristic; it is making those characteristics or abilities functional as part of how the leader acts (his habits) in service to others and applying those characteristics (beyond just having them) in personal and service relations to others. The character or known characteristic defines some aspects of your abilities or who you are inside— e.g. honest, humble, brave, etc. Your attribute, on the other hand, defines your habits; a display of how you use your characteristics, or the actions you exhibit toward others because of who you are inside. For example, empathy as a leadership characteristic becomes a leadership attribute if the followers can distinguish the leader's acts or habits of empathy, such as walking through with his followers in their state of suffering to bring wholeness; otherwise, it is just a characteristic or ability. Leadership attributes toward others are what impact the followers' and the organizational growth more than ability and competence.

In addressing one of the self-righteous hypocritical attributes of servitude leadership, Jesus called leader-servants to be "inside-out" leaders that reflect credibility; indeed, leaders should not appear outwardly righteous when they are full of hypocrisy and lawlessness in their hearts. He was describing "inside–out" as an authentic leadership attribute measured by the display of credibility a leadership attribute! The measuring stick of a leader-servant is Jesus Christ. We measure ourselves unto the measure of the status of the fullness of Christ (Ephesians 4:13).

The leadership attributes of an authentic leader as a servant are encapsulated in **SERVANT/SERVING LEADERSHIP** are listed in Table 1.1, and defined in Table 1.2: *Servanthood, Emulation, Responsibility, Vision, Navigation, Adaptability, Trust, Listening, Empathy, Affection, Discipleship, Encouragement, Reproduction, Stewardship, Healing-Care, Initiation, Integrity,* and *Persuasion*. Other support attributes include *Influence, Courage, and Generosity*.

The attributes have been separated into Outward and Outbound (Inner Strength) leadership Attributes. As shown in Table 1.1, each of these attributes has three or more leadership characteristics. As such, more than 65 leadership characteristics are covered in these 20 attributes. For example, a leader's Servanthood leadership attribute is characterized by his willing servant's heart of selfless role humility, sacrifice, and submissiveness. The more these are present in a leader, the more effective the servant leadership.

Table 1.1: The functional leader-servant leadership Outbound (Inner Strength) and Outward attributes

	LEADER-SERVANT LEADERSHIP ATTRIBUTES			INNER STRENGTH ATTRIBUTES	OUTWARD ATTRIBUTES
S	Servanthood	L	Listening	Adaptability	Affection
E	Emulation	E	Empathy	Courage	Discipleship
R	Responsibility	A	Affection	Empathy	Emulation
V	Vision	D	Discipleship	Encouragement	Generosity
A	Adaptability	E	Encouragement	Initiation	Healing–Care
N	Navigation	R	Reproduction	Listening	Influence
T	Trust	S	Stewardship	Navigation	Persuasion
I	Influence	H	Healing–Care	Responsibility	Reproduction
G	Generosity	I	Initiation	Stewardship	Servanthood
C	Courage	P	Persuasion	Vision	Trust/Integrity

The list does not assume that a leader has to be excellent in all attributes or even have all of them to be an effective Leader–Servant.

However, the more of these attributes the leader displays in his acts of service toward others, the more productive he or she will be, and the further his impact on the followers and organization. The table also shows that two or more attributes can share common characteristics, which can be applied or observed in different contexts. For example, a leader's ability to inspire followers can be seen in his acts of discipleship, empowerment, an.d encouragement attributes in the context in which these attributes apply. Each attribute is exhibited either as a part of the outbound inner strength attribute of a leader or a part of the outward attribute. Table 1.1 is not an exhaustive list of attributes; in fact, there are hundreds of such attributes. This is just the starting point.

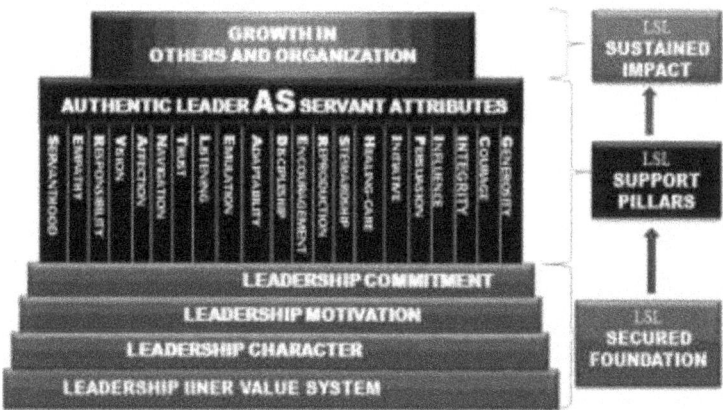

Figure 1.2: Servant leadership outward attributes (dark blue) and relationship to four foundational layers of the LSL Model

Figure 1.2 shows that the leader's attributes are shaped and secured by his four foundational layers (leadership inner value system, leadership character, motivation, and commitment). The attributes of the leader–servants are also conceptualized as the support pillars that will establish and support the personal authenticity of the leader, what the leader, does and the effectiveness of the leadership process. Thus, the attributes represent functional pillars of authentic leadership that can be learned or enriched as described in detail in the subsequent chapters. The combined effect of a secured foundation and stable support pillars will make a sustained impact on the growth of followers and the organization.

COMPARISONS WITH OTHER WORKS

The original works by Greenleaf (1970) in servant leadership [1] have been reviewed by Larry Spears (1996), who identified listening, empathy, healing, awareness, persuasion, conceptualization, foresight, stewardship, commitment to the growth of others, and building community as the ten distinguishing characteristics of servant leadership. [2] Russell (2001) has studied these attributes and have shown them to be essential in servant leadership and concluded that these qualities generally "grow out of the inner values and beliefs of individual leaders." [3] Russell and Stone (2002) extended the Greenleaf 10 attributes to 20 attributes observed in servant-leaders. These 20 attributes were categorized by these authors as either functional attributes (intrinsic characteristics of servant-leaders) or accompanying attributes (complement attributes that enhance the functional attributes).[4] The operational attributes were identified as vision, honesty, integrity, trust, modeling, service, pioneering, appreciation, and empowerment with the accompanying attributes of communication, credibility, competence, stewardship, visibility, influence, persuasion, listening, encouragement, teaching, and delegation. Only three of the attributes identified by Greenleaf were identified, and all three were accompanying attributes rather than functional. Responsibility, adaptability, affection, discipleship, navigation, and reproduction attributes which are considered critical in biblical-based servant leadership in my LSL model are not covered by Russell and Greenleaf. As shown in the description of the attributes in Table 1.2, most of the attributes reported by Russell and Stone (2002)[5] or Greenleaf [1] can be seen either in the twenty attributes or their associated characteristics. Integrity and honesty for example are leadership characteristics of trust and other attributes rather than an independent attributes. I take the position that servant leadership attributes are functional attributes in acts of duty to others and emanate from the inner value system of the leader.

CHAPTER 1
UNDERSTANDING LEADERSHIP ATTRIBUTES

Table 1.2: Description of the functional leader-servant outward leadership attributes and associated principles and characteristics

Leader–Servant Leadership Attributes	Principles of Leadership Attributes	Leadership Characteristics
Affection: *This is the combined love-based works toward providing the essential help or services for the spiritual growth or survival of another person. .* (Chapter 2)	*Affection flows from a person to produce positive emotions for the well-being of another person*	Kindness Compassion Practical Love Affective signs Appreciation
Discipleship: *This is the combined acts of personally developing, intentionally equipping, and attentively empowering growth in others to reproduce a heart of service.* (Chapter 3)	*Discipleship transforms and empowers followers for service leadership that grows communities.*	Inspiring Shepherding Equipping Developing Empowering
Emulation: *This is the combined acts of initiating an authentic servant attitude as a model of service worthy of following* (Chapter 4)	*A great leader-servant outwardly and positively inspires a pattern of good works for others to follow.*	Inspiration Motivation Initiation Model Following
Generosity: *This is the combined acts of freely sharing with and giving to others as an act of kindness, without expectation of reward or return to him.* (Chapter 5)	*Generosity is an outward measure of the level of sacrifice, what is shared, or the impact a giving makes, not just the size of the giving.*	Sharing Giving Kindness Affection Love
Healing-Care: *This is the combined acts of providing comfort and empathy to make others whole emotionally and spiritually along with tending to the follower's physical and mental well-being.* (Chapter 6)	*Comforting others in any trouble with the comfort with which we are comforted by God, brings healing - wholeness.*	Self-Healing Empathy Reconciliation Comfort Relational
Influence: *This is the combined acts of positively affecting desired change in conduct,*	*The true measure of leadership success in affecting*	Model Positive attitude Authority

performance, and relational connections toward others-centered course of action or service. (Chapter 7)	desired change in conduct, performance, and relational connections in others is influence	Connection Wisdom Intelligence,
Persuasion: This is the combined acts of communicating perspective to connect, challenge, and convince with a compelling purpose to convert others to a new position. (Chapter 8)	The means of transforming others to a new perspective is through empathetic persuasion	Connecting Challenging Communicating Convincing Converting Encouraging
Reproduction: This is the combined acts of developing your leadership qualities in others and releasing them as successors to continue a greater mission. (Chapter 9)	Great leaders produce successors for legacy and greater courses as an expected product of an effective leadership reproduction.	Selecting Mentoring Equipping Empowering Releasing
Servanthood: This is the combined acts of humility, willingness, and intentionality in service to others through selfless sacrifice and submission as a servant. (Chapter 10)	A leader-servant is most qualified to lead when most ready to serve as a servant for the growth of others. The role of a leader is to serve as a servant	Servant's heart Humility Sacrifice Service Willingness Submissiveness
Trust: This is the combined acts of positive display of character, competence, credibility, and shared relational connections that produce assured trust-confidence of the trustee in the trusted. (Chapter 11)	True leadership trust produces assured trustee's confidence and readiness to follow based on the credibility, competence, and shared relational connections of the trusted.	Character Competence Integrity Credibility Confidence

PRINCIPLE OF LEADERSHIP ATTRIBUTE

In the context of servant leadership, a leadership attribute is a level above the leadership characteristic or trait of a leader. The principle of leadership attribute states that every leadership attribute has a set of distinguishing characteristics that make up the inward or outward display of the attribute. The principle reflects the essential designed purpose or outcome of the attribute or the inevitable consequence of the effective practice of the attribute. Thus, the principle of leadership attribute is a concise statement about the fundamental truth, value, or belief about the attribute in a leadership situation; it is a statement that establishes an idea about the outcome of the attribute for guiding the practical application of the attribute and its characteristics. I will postulate and frame each principle as an additive function of the characteristics of the attribute. A statement of each principle is quoted at the beginning or below the title of each chapter. It is yet to be experimentally proven if the attribute is a linear or some other non-linear function of these characteristics as variables. It is expected, however, that each character will contribute to the effectiveness of the attribute in varying degrees.

AUTHENTIC LEADERSHIP ATTRIBUTES

At a personal level, attributes are the value-based inside-out moral leadership assets that can be related to the authenticity of a leader-servant. The complexity of defining authenticity has been noted in the literature. The subject of authentic leadership is well covered in the works of Terry (1993),[5] George (2003),[6] and Shair and Eilam (2005).[7] All appear to agree that authenticity requires self-awareness and objective self-identity in personal and social interactions with others. In his book, *Advocacy Leadership*, Professor Gary L. Anderson offers individual, organizational, and societal perspectives on authenticity: "Authenticity, at a peculiar level, is living a life, whether in the private or professional term. This is congruent with one's espoused values; at the structural level, authenticity has to do with viewing human beings as ends in themselves, rather than means to other ends; at the public level, it is a state of affairs that is congruous with the shared political and cultural values of society."[8]

The basic tenets of these perspectives are very fitting to authenticity as a qualifying element of leader-servant leadership attributes. The attribute reflects how the followers see the leader based on the leader's distinctive features displayed through his or her actions personally, organizationally, and societally. The leader is seen as a leader-servant or serving leader because the followers see him lead as a servant from an inside-out value of others. This is what makes the leader authentic. Authenticity means that what a leader displays outside, in personal or leadership life of service to others, and society is based on the values the leader espouses inside.

Authenticity in servant leadership can be one or two types or both: *Outbound Authenticity and Outward Authenticity*. The Outbound (outward-bound) Authenticity is the genuineness of personal honesty from your inner strength and abilities; what you say and how you act emanate from who you are or how you feel inside. It reflects the essential truth and honesty about your outward-bound inner strength.

Outward authenticity, on the other hand, describes the truthfulness of your credibility and honesty displayed outward in relation to others; your *outer* visible behavior or how you act outwardly towards others reflects exactly your true intentions.

While *outward* authenticity is the visible *outer* indicator of the truth of who you are inside, *outbound* authenticity is outward-bound attribute from the inside of who you are. Credibility in this context is the influence a leader has to attract believability, trustworthiness, and authenticity; it is the believability, trustworthiness, and authenticity of who you are inside and outside.

A key element of personal authenticity is that it is seen or measured in the context of societal, cultural, and organizational interactions. In that context, achieving individual authenticity becomes a challenge since it is influenced by social factors and dispositions of individuals who usually depend on liberal and organizational realities. However, for leader-servant leadership, the leader can face those changing times by remaining focused on his key Biblical-based principles or *Leadership Inner Value System*. Thus, I am interested in authenticity as an essential element of effective Leader-servant leadership attributes or Leader-servant leadership attributes as drivers of leadership authenticity. With that in mind, the first critical element of authenticity in practicing or developing efficient leader-servant leadership attributes is inside-out self-examination relative to the people served rather than the organization. You may ask yourself: What will be my response when the people I lead act or react in a certain way, will it be negative or positive? What are my strengths and vulnerabilities at those times?

Professor Yacobi in his post, "Elements of Human Authenticity," noted that since "the self -arise attribute emerges from interactions

CHAPTER 1
UNDERSTANDING LEADERSHIP ATTRIBUTES

between self, others, and the environment in a complex society and world, there may co-exist multiple complicated identities depending on place and context." [9] He went on to identify the following <u>essential elements of personal authenticity</u>: self-awareness, unbiased self-examination, accurate self-knowledge, reflective judgment, personal responsibility, and integrity, genuineness, and humility, empathy for others, understanding of others, optimal utilization of feedback from others. All of these are covered under the leadership attributes or characteristics shown in Table 1.2.

Bill George, in his book, *Authentic Leadership*, takes the position that to be an authentic leader; a person must have the following essential characteristics: [10]

- Behavior based on value: He must understand his own values and exhibit behavior to others based on those values;
- He must not compromise his values in difficult situations but could use the situation to strengthen personal values in those situations.
- Passion from a clear purpose: Be self-aware of who he is, where he is going, and the right thing to do.
- Compassion from the heart: He must lead from a compassionate heart that allows them to be sensitive to the plight and needs of others,
- Connectedness from a relationship; he must be relationally connected with people he leads,
- Consistency from the self-disciple: He must demonstrate self-discipline to remain calm, collected, and consistent in a stressful situation.

Modeled after the elements above, Table 1.3 lists six essential characteristics of authenticity for servant leadership. These fundamental characteristics cover the five identified above and can also be aligned with the leadership characteristics in Table 1.2. Each attribute in Table 1.2 is expected to pass the personal authenticity test in Tables 1.3, 1.4. In a survey of 132 Christian leaders, seventy-four percent (74%) of them agreed that they always or frequently exhibit servant leadership attributes. [11] Thus, a pass of the outward authenticity test means that a pure leader must demonstrate 70% or more of these essential elements of this legitimacy. (That is, 70% YES in the assessment questions in Tables 1.3, 1.4).

It needs to be noted, however, that a secular leader could be authentic and still lack some of the essential servant leadership attributes or characteristics such as selflessness, servanthood, and love-motivated servant attitudes of a leader-servant. Effective leader-servants are authentic leaders and personal authenticity is an essential element of leader-servant leadership. The key test for leader-servant authenticity is the quality of his inside-out value and personal character. What is most important is a change from the inside-out.

	Table 1.3: The test of essential elements of personal inner strength authenticity in servant leadership		
	Elements of Inner Strength Authenticity	**Inner Strength (Outbound) Authenticity Assessment Questions**	**YES / NO**
1	Personal inside-out value-based behavior	Are your personal inside-out values aligned with acts of service and behavior outside?	1
		Are you honest to yourself in relation to your inner strengths and abilities?	2
2	Inside-out Self-Awareness	Do you have unbiased self-examination, and accurate self-knowledge of who you are inside-out?	3
		Do you know your inner strength and weaknesses in relation to the good you want to show as an outward attribute?	4
3	Inside-out Empathy-Compassion	Do you know and feel from your inside what you want for your followers?	5
		Are you motivated to empathize, based on your inside feelings?	6
4	Inside-out Connection with followers	Do you feel deep, personal, and spiritual connection with your followers?	7
		Does what you say and how you act reflect how you feel when you relate to others?	8
5	Inside-out Emotional Self-regulation	Do you have difficulty controlling your emotion in order to remain calm in a stressful situation?	9
		Are you always able to comfort yourself?	10
6	Inside-out Authenticity Feedback	Do your followers see your inside-out value from your outside behavior?	11
		Will your followers feel that what you say you are is congruent with how you act?	12
	#YESs_____ ; # NOs_____ : Outbound Authenticity: YES/ 12————%		

CHAPTER 1
UNDERSTANDING LEADERSHIP ATTRIBUTES

	Table 1.4: The test of essential elements of personal outward authenticity in servant leadership		
	Elements of Personal Outward Authenticity	Personal Outward Authenticity Assessment Questions	YES or NO
1	Personal value-based outward behavior	Are your personal values and beliefs aligned with your acts of service and behavior toward others?	1
		Do you live out your life according to your beliefs?	2
2	Personal Self-Awareness	Do you have clarity of your personal vision and purpose?	3
		Does what you know about yourself accurately describe what others say?	4
3	Personal Outward Empathy-Compassion	Do you apply how you feel to what your followers need?	5
		Do you lead from a compassionate heart and are you sensitive to the plight and needs of others?	6
4	Personal Connection with followers	Do you feel deep, personal connection with your followers?	7
		Does your outward action toward others reflect exactly your true intentions?	8
5	Outward Emotional Self-regulation	Do you have difficulty controlling your emotions to remain calm in a stressful situation?	9
		Does your evaluation of your value of others agree with how valued they feel?	10
6	Personal Authenticity Feedback	Do your followers see your outward acts as true and honest?	11
		Can your followers see other-centeredness in 70% or more of your attributes?	12
#YESs_____; # NOs_____; Outward Authenticity: YES/ 12————%			

ALS EMULATION LEADERSHIP
ATTRIBUTES, PRINCIPLES, & PRACTICES

Table 1.5. Leader As Servant-Leadership Audit

A servant-leader in his leadership position purposefully choses to serve and inspire acts of service in others by his example. Select and circle best answer to questions
1=Never; 2=Almost never; 3=Sometimes; 4=Frequently; 5 =Always

	Servant Leadership assessment questions	Circle no				
1	I am willing and other-centered, and readily chose to serve others as a servant for their personal growth	1	2	3	4	5
2	I model others-centered attitude in my service and relationships and inspire same for others to follow	1	2	3	4	5
3	I have a sense of obligation, willingness, and accountability for the service towards others	1	2	3	4	5
4	I have the foresightedness to specify in the present view what others' growth should be in a given future	1	2	3	4	5
5	I work toward providing the essential help or services for the spiritual growth or survival of the others;	1	2	3	4	5
6	I provide the needed purposeful course of action for how to chart the course to for my followers.	1	2	3	4	5
7	I display external credibility and a strong sense of character based on values, beliefs, and competence;	1	2	3	4	5
8	In communication, I attentively perceive and hear what is communicated, reflectively listen to understand and to be understood	1	2	3	4	5
9	I walk through with others in their state (suffering, emotions, etc.) in a way that provides the needed care and well-being	1	2	3	4	5
10	I have a measure of self-secured flexibility to adapt appropriate attitude to serve all people in different situations	1	2	3	4	5
11	I personally develop, intentionally equip, and attentively nurture spiritually growth in others	1	2	3	4	5
12	My act of bravery instills in others the courage and confidence to follow or persevere in a course of action	1	2		4	5
13	I develop my leadership qualities in others as successors to continue in a purposeful mission	1	2	3	4	5
14	I manage, maintain,, and account for all resources entrusted to me and being responsible for the difference my acts make	1	2	3	4	5
15	As a care-giver, I act to comfort and make others whole emotionally	1	2	3	4	5
16	When I see a need, I originate a vision and action, and stay committed to meet that need and desired change	1	2	3	4	5

CHAPTER 1
UNDERSTANDING LEADERSHIP ATTRIBUTES

17	I display a holistic view of an issue to inform, transform or convert others to my view through empathetic persuasion	1	2	3	4	5
18	I freely share what I have sacrificially as an act of kindness to others, without expectation of reward in return	1	2	3	4	5
19	My act of influence is to affect the actions, behavior, opinions, etc., of others based on trust, credibility and relationship	1	2	3	4	5
20	In the face challenges and danger, I act with bravery to overcome fear and take a stand with strength and conviction	1	2	3	4	5
Score Range	Add up the numbers in each column (Total Score____ Check and Understand the key areas to work on					
81-100	Strong Leader-Servant; keep it up, go and train others.					
66-80	Above average Leader-Servant; work 25% of key areas					
50-65	Average but developing; need to work on 50% of key areas					
34-49	Below average leader; work on 75% of key areas					
<34	Not a Leader-Servant; need training in all areas					

Summary 1
Understanding Leadership Process

Before starting this exercise, please read and follow the instruction in the preface of this workbook. Answers to these questions are contained in this chapter. Completion of these exercises after reading the chapter should take 60-90 minutes.

Discovering the Leadership Attributes

1. What is your alternative definition of leadership? In learning to lead, how would you differentiate the following elements:
    a. Leadership,
    b. Leader as servant leadership.
    c. Leadership characteristics.
    d. Leadership attributes
2. How should you lead in the context of this chapter?

ALS EMULATION LEADERSHIP
ATTRIBUTES, PRINCIPLES, & PRACTICES

Understanding the Leadership Principles

1. Define or state the principle of Servanthood Leadership attribute. How true is that in your leadership experience?
2. What are the key differences between the Leader as Servant and the Servant as Leader Leadership philosophies?
3. How can you display the essential qualities of authentic leader in a leadership process in challenging times.?
4. What are the characteristics of a leader-servant?
5. What was the original source of the Servant as Leader (SL)? What was the original source of Leader as Servant (LS)?
6. How do you compare the two model characters of Leo in SL and Jesus in LS
7. What is the key framework of a Leader as a Servant Leadership?

Practicing Authentic Leadership

1. Authenticity in servant leadership can be one or two types or both *Outbound Authenticity and Outward Authenticity*. Describe a time when you displayed:
    a. The Outbound (outward-bound)— *outbound* authenticity is outward-bound attribute from the inside of who you are.
    b. *The Outward Authenticity*—*outward* authenticity is the visible *outer* indicator of the truth of who you are inside,
2. Describe the key elements of personal authenticity seen or measured in the context of societal, cultural, and organizational interactions.
3. Take the outbound (Table 1.3) and Outward (Table 1.4) leadership authenticity tests. How (%) authentic are you (#YES/12) in each measure in your leadership process?
4. In the elements you rated as NO, review the relevant passage, learn what is missing in you and write a personal commitment statement on how to work to improve in those areas
5. How much of a leader-servant are you? Take the personal leader-servant audit in Table 1.5 to self-assess your effectiveness.
6. Based on the questions in Table 1.5, can you identify each of the twenty attributes? What ones did you score 3 ("sometimes") or less than 3? Review and learn and commit to work to improve.

CHAPTER 2
LEADERSHIP EMULATION ATTRIBUTE

A great leader-servant outwardly and positively inspires a pattern of good works for others to follow.

To emulate is to strive to be like someone else or to follow someone else's example by imitating something that inspires you about that person. Have you ever emulated someone—your teacher, your father, or your mother? How did you use what you learned from following the footstep of your hero to grow to where you are today? Jesus in the scripture above modeled humility and Servanthood he wanted his disciples to develop. As a leader, how do you model a characteristic behavior for someone to follow or develop? How is Leadership Emulation an outward leadership attribute? This chapter explores these and other questions to discover the characteristics of emulation attributes and to formulate a functional principle based on the expected outcome of effective use of these attributes in leadership.

CHARACTERISTICS OF EMULATION ATTRIBUTE

Emulation as a leadership attribute shares some characteristics with transformative leadership, where a leader intentionally conveys a clear vision of a goal, inspires the passion for the work toward the goal, and motivates the followers to follow. The key to emulation is the level of moral motivation and perception for the work, and passion to work towards common goals that the leader wants for the followers. The emulation attribute is an outward attribute. As an element of trans-formative leadership, the emulation attribute allows a leader to outwardly exhibit the following desired behaviors he wants followers to imitate. Professor Bernard M. Bass identified the four elements of transformational leadership as: [18]

(1) *Intellectual Stimulation* – allowing the leader to encourage followers to explore and discover brand new ways of doing and learning things;
(2) *Individualized Consideration* –involving the leader offering help and encouragement to fellow followers and fostering supportive relationships;
(3) *Inspirational Motivation* –the leader having a clear vision that they are can articulate to followers and competent to help followers experience the same passion and motivation to fulfill the new goals; and
(4) *Idealized Influence* – the leader serving as a role model for followers to emulate and internalize his ideas through the trust and respect they have garnished for the leader.

According to Bass and Riggio, in their text, *Transformational Leadership:* Transformational leaders stimulate and inspire followers to both achieve extraordinary outcomes and, in the process, develop their leadership capacity… help followers grow and develop into leaders by responding to individual followers' needs by empowering them and by aligning the objectives and goals of the distinctive followers, the leader, the group, and the larger organization.[19]

What does the scripture teach about emulation for the transformation of followers to learn new things or follow in a mission? A leader's ability to emulate Christ is a critical outward attribute of servant leadership. In John, we read; "'do you understand what I have done for you?' (…) *Now* that I, your Lord and Teacher, have washed your feet, you also should wash one another's feet" (John 13:12-14, NIV). What does it mean for a leader to lead others by emulating someone else? The phrase "what I have done for you" refers to the example Jesus showed the disciples. It is about them as followers or leaders-in-training emulating the Master, they see to allow them to follow the same goal.

Chapter 2
Leadership Emulation Attributes

There's a very clear alignment of these four elements of transformation leadership to the scripture above. Emulation in servant leadership is a process that takes four critical actions that Jesus took:

1) Intellectual Stimulation – allowing the leader to encourage followers to explore and discover brand new ways of doing and learning things;
2) With the inspired heart to serve, He initiated (pursued a goal) actions to show how to begin to serve.
3) This is carried out by actually walking the walk and modeling the initiative with practical examples others can follow.
4) The process ends by challenging or giving the new leader-servant the responsibility to follow and live out the example with others. Emulation was a command, not a choice for leader-servants: "…you also should wash one another's feet" (John 13:12-14).

In this example, Jesus showed that the first requirement to emulate servant ministry is to be an absolute servant or adopt child-like humility. He also showed that He cared about His disciple's personal and group needs for development. This is similar to what could be the general outcome of trans-formative leadership. According to Professor Bernard M. Bass, "Transformational leaders hold positive expectations for followers, believing that they can do their best. As a result, they inspire, empower, and stimulate followers to exceed normal levels of performance"[20]

Principle of Emulation Attribute

The distinguishing leadership characteristics of emulation attribute are the leader's acts of Inspiration, Initiation, *Modeling, and Following*, leading me to the following functional definition:

Servant leadership emulation attribute is the combined acts of initiating an authentic servant attitude as a model of service worthy of following as an example.

The primary outcome of the emulation attribute is to lead others by substantial example outwardly displayed for others to follow. Authentic examples that have been tested and irrefutably proven to be reliable over time and situations are those of Jesus Christ. The Apostle Paul was a leader who closely followed Jesus' examples and inspired followers in his world and ours with those experiences. Here is the principle:

Servant leadership emulation principle: A great leader servant outwardly and positively inspires a pattern of good works for others to follow.

This principle means that to be a great leader you must be willing to follow, learn, and pattern your growth after the best leader-Jesus in service to others. Leading by emulation is inspiring and motivating the followers to observe your intentions and how and why they (followers) should follow your example as the leader. The following additive formula illustrates the process:

INSPIRATION + INITIATION +MODELING+ FOLLOWING = EMULATION

The process is shown in Figure 4 as a cyclic sequence of actions that build on each other to display emulation attributes.

The model also shows that the acts of emulation can occur directly without a sequence. For example, one can lead others to follow by the independent act of emulation-inspiration or by any of the other characteristics. The sum of any or all the actions is emulation to follow an example of service to others.

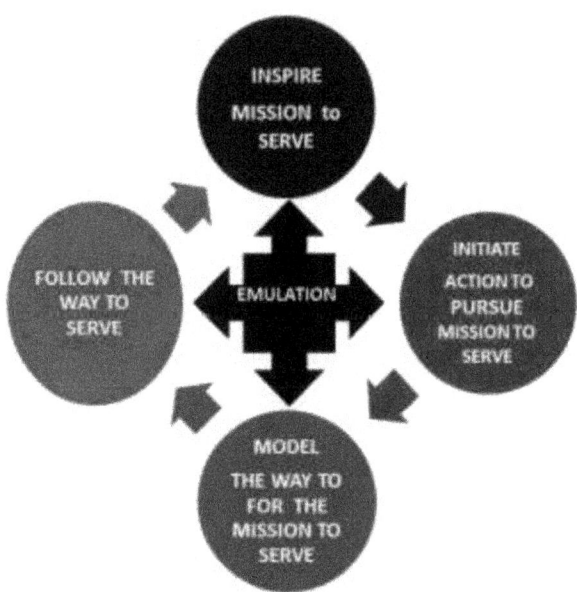

Figure 4: Model of servant leadership emulation attribute

Summary 2
Leadership Emulation Attribute

Before starting this exercise, please read and follow the instruction in the preface of this workbook. Answers to these questions are contained in this chapter. Completion of these exercises after reading the chapter should take 60-90 minutes.

Discovering the Acts of emulation leadership Attribute

1. Define emulation? Illustrate your definition with example where you emulate someone. How did you use what you learned?
2. How is Leadership Emulation an outward leadership attribute?
3. What are the distinguishing leadership characteristics of emulation attribute
4. How is emulation attribute an element of transformative leadership proposed by Bass [18]
5. What does the scripture teach about emulation for the transformation of followers? (John 13:12-14, NIV).

Principle of Emulation Attribute

1. What are four critical action you can take in emulation in servant leadership process that Jesus took (John 13:12-14).
2. As a leader, how do you model a characteristic behavior for someone to follow or develop?
3. How did Jesus model emulation in his Servanthood example he wanted his disciples to develop?

Practicing Emulation-Attribute (Ch. 4)

1. What would you consider the key characteristics of emulation leadership attributes?
2. How many acts of emulation as an attribute do you display?
3. Take the Leadership Emulation Attribute audit in Table 12.4.

Principle of Emulation Leadership Attribute

1. *Define Servant leadership emulation attribute*

2. What is the primary outcome of the emulation attribute How did Apostle Paul demonstrate Emulation leadership?
3. State the principle of *Servant leadership emulation principle:*
4. What does this principle mean if you want to be a great leader?
5. State the additive law of emulation attribute
6. What does the model of emulation in Figure 2.1 sow about sequence of acts of emulation

CHAPTER 3
DEVELOPING THE ACTS OF EMULATION-INSPIRATION

To inspire or motivate is to influence someone to do something. Jesus' humility inspired His followers to emulate him. First, his Humility inspired the intentions (the goal) and desire to serve. Then, the process of initiation sets up the actions to pursue the outstanding goal. Self-efficacy translates inspired intentions into initiating actions or desiring to pursue the goal. Emulation - inspiration refers to those actions designed to motivate someone to follow the example.

INSPIRATION BY A DESIRE TO IMITATE CHRIST

A leader is inspired by a desire to imitate Christ's example to serve others. This requires the leader to work on several aspects of his life to train his character. Some of the attitudes the leader must have are his love for mankind. This is the quality of humility in his character and his understanding of what it takes to be a servant; his self-efficacy (one's belief in his or her power to produce an effect or competence in him- or herself or others). The self-efficacy of a leader forms not only the behavioral intentions and develops action plans but initiates actions as well.

To increase the leader's ability to lead by emulation, the followers first need to be inspired by observing intentions and why they should be motivated to follow the example. People often need to see something to believe in a leader they want to follow. In some cases, people follow the agenda or what the person stands for and is inspired by knowledge of what they want or observe in the leader.

What are other elements or desires that can inspire us to take action to emulate Christ-likeness? Some elements (such as convictions, values, and love) inspire us to lead by emulation because they reinforce our feelings and need to care for others and train us to be better leader-servants. Knowing that your success as a leader-servant by emulation depends on your ability and desire to imitate Christ-likeness should motivate you to identify key elements and activities that lead you to emulate. Here are a few elements that our desire to emulate Christ-likeness can motivate:

Desire to emulate Christ-likeness is inspired by His humility. Jesus' actions to inspire his disciples were to show them, even though he was their leader, that he was humble, secure enough, and willing to be a servant. His position, which the disciples considered to be most important, was least important to Him.

Desire to emulate Christ-likeness is inspired by your love to serve. The core of Jesus' Servanthood was that he was motivated by love to serve others. His selfless love drove Him to serve others. We need to see the love for each person from the perspective of indescribable God's love for us as leaders. See the opportunities you have as a leader as a privilege to serve others, not as a right for your position. That realization creates a sense of humility to love and a desire to serve others.

Desire to emulate Christ-likeness motivates your actions to give up rights and pride. The disciples could not be humble enough to be the least if their self-worth was more important than serving others. By doing good deeds, the humility of a servant's heart exposes pride in others. Peter's pride would not allow him to see how the Jesus that he knew to be God could stoop ignoble enough to serve him. A leader must possess a sense of security if he is serving and empowering others; Jesus' sense of security enabled him to be humble and to stoop low in service to others.

Instruction

The following set of questions is designed to serve as a guide to discover, explore, and practice the essential ALS leadership attributes, principles, and practices in leadership process. The questions are comprehensive review based on the content of this chapter only.

To maximize the learning outcomes, the learner must read through this chapter and sections. Some referenced scriptures in the book are repeated in the summaries for added review if needed, even though they were discussed in the section in which they apply.

CHAPTER 3
DEVELOPING THE ACTS OF EMULATION-INSPIRATION

All answers to the questions are contained in the associated chapter or sections; consultation of new sources is not needed. Thus, it is expected that you answer the questions after you have read the book.

SUMMARY 3
DEVELOPING THE ACTS OF EMULATION-INSPIRATION

Before starting this exercise, please read and follow the instruction in the preface of this workbook. Answers to these questions are contained in this chapter. Completion of these exercises after reading the chapter should take 60-90 minutes.

Discovering the Acts of Emulation-Inspiration

1. What does it mean to inspire or motivate?
2. What inspired Jesus' followers to follow to emulate Him
3. What are other elements or desires that can inspire us to take action to emulate Christ-likeness

Principle of Emulation leadership Attribute

1. Your success as a leader-servant by emulation depends on your ability and desire to imitate Christ-likeness should motivate you to identify key elements and activities that lead you to emulate.
2. Identify a few elements that your desire to emulate Christ-likeness can motivate

Practicing Acts of Emulation Leadership Attribute

Emulation-Emulation is defined as the inspirations focused on providing a motive to influence somebody to do something.

1. How can your humility inspire others to want to emulate you?
2. How can others desire to emulate you, be inspired by your humility, Love to serve, and be motivated to sacrifice to serve?
3. What does it require in a follower to cultivate the desire or increase ability to lead by emulation?

CHAPTER 4
DEVELOPING THE ACTS OF EMULATION-INITIATION

Emulation-Initiation refers to the process or attitude of translating intents or goals into actions to emulate. Motivation or inspiration may create behavioral intent or lead you to set a goal, but it takes volition or initiation to pursue that goal or translate the intent into action. Initiation as a step above motivation or inspiration means translating intended goals into action. For example, Jesus motivated His disciples by showing them the need to serve others but initiated the intent in their hearts when he stooped to wash their feet. A such vivid initiative created an indelible picture of His action in their hearts. Here are a few examples of initiation in emulation:

INITIATE A DESIRE TO EMULATE YOUR OWN WILL

How did Paul initiate young Timothy into emulating him in servant leadership ministry? The Apostle Paul describes in 1 and 2 Timothy how he sent Timothy to lead the church in Ephesus by his own will. Just as Jesus lead them by example, Paul initiated servant ministry in Timothy by willfully providing the opportunity for Timothy to emulate him. Paul motivated Timothy by showing him respect and love even though he knew his junior age might be a problem for some members of the Ephesian church. Paul encouraged Timothy by telling him not to let anyone look down on him because he was young. Instead, Paul told Timothy to lead by example in five areas. He said; "Let no one despise you for your youth, but set the believers an example in speech, in conduct, in love, in faith, in purity" (1 Timothy 4:12, ESV). Paul also showed Timothy specific principles of leadership to imitate. Five areas in which you can be an example by your own will are:

Initiate a desire to emulate in your speech and conversations. How we say things and what we say in conversations reflect much about the intent of our hearts, our feelings, and our emotions. The

Bible says that out of the abundance of our hearts, the mouth speaks (Matthew 12:34, NKJV). So, we must guide our tongue to be an excellent example of good works in Christ. Be sensitive to the feelings of others in the words you use, your body language, your tone of voice, and so on. Furthermore, strive to be self-controlled to regulate your emotions when dealing with offensive situations.

Initiate a desire to emulate your conduct. Our conduct in life (defined as how we choose to live our lives) is one of the most important external cues that people use to judge our integrity as an example of Christ. If you teach the Word, do you live what you teach? Does your life reflect Christ-likeness? Does your life in private and public reflect what you really profess to be?

Initiate a desire to emulate your acts of love. Love is defined by what it does in our relationships with people and God. Our love is a direct reflection of the love of God. It is a total contradiction to say you love God and yet not show love to your brethren or your spouse. The primary requirement of a leader-servant is to love and serve others. It is impracticable to serve others without having selfless, other-centered love, which will come from inside you. Without such love, it is impossible to be motivated to take care of others as a servant. The love of Christ, which is deeply rooted in our hearts, will reflect outside us to impact others. Such love can hardly be hidden.

Initiate a desire to emulate in your exercise of faith. How we exercise our faith and how we give glory to God for what he does in our lives says a lot about us as leaders. For example, many years ago when I was a student, all I had was my faith. I had unwavering faith in the promises of God that I had no room to be sad, even when we had nothing to eat. God had a way of showing up to meet our needs. It was important for me to have lived a life of faith in the Lord. I knew people who confessed that they honored the invitation to attend the African Christian fellowship to which I belonged because of the passion with which I testified to God's goodness. Living by faith to me means living on unwavering faith in what Christ can do and sharing that testimony of God's work with others, giving him all the glory.

Initiate a desire to emulate your purity. Purity is the state of being free from anything that debases, contaminates, or pollutes our lives, souls, thoughts, and beliefs. Believers and leader-servants, in particular, are called to purity. This means staying far from sin in all of its forms and things that easily lead us to sin against God. We keep ourselves pure by guarding our way according to God's word (Psalms 119:9), by confessing our sins (1 John 1:9), by living the fruits of the spirit (Galatians 5:19-22), and by staying away from sinful desires and temptations.

Initiate the desire to emulate personal examples of good works. A leader must not pursue what he can attract or model by the pattern of his life. "But seek first the kingdom of God and His righteousness, and all these things shall be added to you" (Matthew 6:33, NKJV). A leader is the light of the world and lightens his immediate environment. As a light, the leader reflects a pattern that attracts others for work and safety. When a light loses or diminishes the power that sustains its ability to shine, an opening door in which darkness may come is created... A leader is also the salt of the earth and his environment. This means that he gives flavor and knowledge to wherever he is and whatever he does. When salt loses its saltiness; "It is no longer good for anything, except to be thrown out and trampled underfoot" (Matthew 5:13-14, NIV). When these qualities of light and salt are present in a leader, he or she will attract those who do not want to be in darkness and those who want to be blessed. Paul, in writing to Titus as he did to Timothy highlighted what is important:

> Encourage young men to live wisely. And you yourself must be an example to them by doing good works of every kind. Let everything you do reflect the integrity and seriousness of your teaching. Teach the truth so that your teaching can't be criticized. Then those who oppose us will be ashamed and have nothing bad to say about us (Titus 2:7-8, NLT).

In everything you do as a leader, show good work through personal examples. The above Scripture demonstrates an excellent pattern to follow:

SEVEN PATTERNS FOR GOOD WORKS:

- *In the mission.* A leader-servant's purpose is to emulate good examples; you must understand what it means to lead by emulation. Paul's purpose was to teach Titus the way to lead by example.

- ***In the model.*** The scripture says, "You yourself must be an example to them" (Titus 2:7, NLT) by doing (initiating) good works. Paul was exemplifying to Titus some of his core leadership principles.
- ***In the mandate.*** Your command is to reflect the integrity and seriousness of your teaching in everything you do. In teaching doctrine, you must maintain the integrity of the Word of God and not compromise with what it says; in reverence, give glory only to God.
- ***In the message.*** Your message is the life and the truth of the Word of God, which you must teach; *"So that your teaching can't be criticized" (Titus 2: 8).*
- ***In the method.*** The method of delivering the truth is sound teaching and living the truth of what you impart.
- ***In the means.*** Use tools effectively (teach the truth) for the mission. Are your works of every kind the means to an end? Do they reflect your integrity?
- ***In the measure.*** Your yardstick for a measure is Jesus Christ. How are you manifesting His life? Are you doing all things for the glory of God? What kind of fruit are you producing and teaching that "Can't be criticized?" (Titus 2:8)

SUMMARY 4
DEVELOPING THE ACTS OF EMULATION-INITIATION

Before starting this exercise, please read and follow the instruction in the preface of this workbook. Answers to these questions are contained in this chapter. Completion of these exercises after reading the chapter should take 60-90 minutes.

Discover Acts of Emulation-Initiation

Define emulation-Initiation.
Emulation-Initiation is defined as an element of motivation for translating the intended goals into action.

CHAPTER 4
DEVELOPING THE ACTS OF EMULATION-INITIATION

1. How can you initiate the desire in others to emulate in the exercise of good choice, in your speech and conservations; your own conduct ; your acts of Love; your exercise of Faith; and your purity,
2. How are personal examples of good works worthy of emulation by others?
3. What role does initiation play in the process of acts of emulation

Principle of emulation Leadership ttribute

As a principle, in everything you do as a leader, show good work through personal examples. Let everything you do reflect the integrity and seriousness of your teaching. Titus 2:7-8, NLT). What seven Patterns for Good works do this scripture demonstrate?

Practicing initiation in emulation:

1. How did Paul initiate young Timothy into emulating him in servant leadership ministry? (1 Timothy and 2 Timothy) How did Paul motivate Timothy and Titus
2. In what five areas did Paul instruct Timothy to lead by example" (1 Timothy 4:12, ESV). Paul also showed Timothy specific principles of leadership to imitate.
3. **Initiate the desire to emulate personal examples of good works. In the context of Matthew 6:33 what does,** "a leader must not pursue what he can attract or model by the pattern of his life."

CHAPTER 5
DEVELOPING THE ACTS OF EMULATION-MODELING

Emulation-model refers to showing a pattern of example and how to emulate. A leader modeling the way to follow gives followers specific examples or pictures of how to pursue the goal of serving. After a servant model ministry was initiated in their hearts, the disciples had to follow Jesus' example of leadership. Jesus took time to show the disciples an example of ministering before giving them the reason for serving them. He taught them responsibility by giving them the responsibility to serve each other. And, most importantly, he taught Servanthood by showing them the way, pointing to the cross, and the importance of serving humanity.

When we model as someone or emulate another person, what exactly do we model or emulate from that person? When Paul said, "Be imitators of me as I am of Christ" (1 Corinthians 11:1, ESV) what was he talking about? He was informing them that his model is Christ and therefore, urging them to imitate him, as long as he also is following the Master Jesus. Paul here is leading by emulation through modeling after Christ. Peter, speaking about leadership, instructed that a leader-servant needs to; "Shepherd the flock of God which is among you, serving as overseers, not by compulsion but willingly, not for dishonest gain but eagerly; nor as being lords over those entrusted to you, but being examples to the flock" (1 Peter 5:2-3). The Leader-Servant must disciple followers by being an example to them in every form. The growth of a local church or fellowship is the product of its spiritual well-being and relationships among members.

Overseeing the flock means being accountable for managing the welfare of the followers, including their growth, spiritual well-being, physical needs, and so on. The emphasis in Peter's letter falls on the character of the overseer being willing to serve, to be other-centered, to take on Servanthood, and to be an exemplar. In the same way, the Apostle Paul's letters to Timothy (Timothy 1 and 2 and Titus) consist of what can be referred to as a leadership training manual regarding discipleship by modeling Christ-likeness. Just as in Peter, it is more of a manual on training the character and the external reputation of leaders among believers and unbelievers than it is training to acquire needed skills. The standards of measure are to be above reproach (1 Timothy 3:2), blameless (1 Timothy 3:10), and self-controlled and upright (Titus 2; 12). We also see Paul with Silas and Timothy personally reaching out to believers in discipleship even though they ministered with one focus to lead each person in the group of believers to follow Christ-likeness.

STRATEGIES TO MODEL EMULATION

Leaders model emulation by practical example. A leader asking followers to do anything he is not willing to do himself sets a double standard. As a leader-servant, you must be diligent in practicing what you preach. Your actions must speak far more than words, and way beyond any training; certainly greater than any employee manual. The actions you take give the follower a direct picture of what to do and how to do it. Effective leaders become what they want their followers to become or live the lifestyle they want their followers to subsist. They model faith and perseverance by living on sound principles. We see these points in the life of Paul: "I can do all things through Christ, who strengthens me" (Philippians 4:13). Leader-servants live out their own responsibilities in each promise of God; "Know that in all things, God works for the good of those who love him, who have been called according to his purpose" (Romans 8:28). Hence, they exemplify God's love through service to others and depend solely on the strength that comes from their faith in God.

Leaders model emulation by leading their community of followers. The Leaders model emulation is by leading your community of followers. What a leader wants for his followers can be related to what he wants for the organization. However, there is a difference. When a leader over-emphasizes what the organization wants and neglects what the individual needs, it leads to conflicts. In such cases, individuals can become disengaged. So, a leader must think of the organization as a collection of people while still respecting individual needs. A corporate body survives only if each member of the organization is engaged to do their part. Here are some tips that an organizational leader must consider:

- Remain positive about the organization to followers.
- Defend the organization's integrity even as you guide the followers to honor the organization's rules.
- Avoid wasting company resources as you positively make the organization sensitive to the need of individuals.
- Be the first to show meaningful sacrifice to grow the organization before you influence others to do the same.
- Set a positive tone of how to achieve desired results for the organizations by being SMART—Strategic, measurable, achievable, reasonable, tractable, and time-bound.

Leaders model the act of emulation by leading a team of leaders. For servant leadership to work from top to bottom and to impact all, it is crucial for the leader to communicate the concepts to everyone in the leadership team. If the head leads by example but the next highest level of leadership does not, the impact will not be effective from top to bottom. It is, therefore, important to inculcate servant leadership concepts in all in the team by publicly living the example. When Jesus washed the disciple's feet in the inner room, He prepared and communicated to them the importance of servant leadership. They understood what he was teaching. The leader-servant example must consistently count throughout the organization.

Leaders model the way to emulate as parents. Being a leader-servant is living a life that's totally devoted to others and worthy of following. As a parent, do you train your children by example? Leaders lead by example by modeling their beliefs and intentions through practical and personal actions. Do these actions match what you say you believe? That is, with the Word of God? Modeling desired leadership behavior can be compared to good parenting. When you really think about it, your followers, like Timothy and Titus in the case of Paul, could be very young and inexperienced. In several instances, Paul referred to Timothy and Titus as my son Timothy or my son Titus. We also read David instructing his son: "My son, give me thine heart, and let thine eyes observe my ways" in Proverbs 23:26 (KJV). In the presence of followers, the leaders must become what they want the followers to be.

Leaders model the attitude they desire in followers. As with a child, if you want your followers to be honorable and completely truthful, punctual, and thorough, then you must let them hear or see you extol these virtues. If you want them to be successful, show them how to be flourishing by demonstrating qualities that lead to success. For example, I have been in a community of followers in which some individuals can only initiate action to change their position when they see you move or show them how. For the sake and growth of the community, show your followers how.

To show your followers how to choose their inner circle of friends, you must not be careless or be yoked with unfruitful friends and co-workers. Indeed, you must show forth in your life how you want your followers to live and be transparent and authentic. You must demonstrate how significance can only be found in your new life and in being a servant to a good master such as Jesus; demonstrate God's love by sharing your testimony. Effective spiritual leaders plant the Word of God and provide clear tools to run the race of leadership.

You must also model a way to emulate decision-making Allow your followers to follow along in your decision-making process, in both words and examples. Explain to them why you came to a particular resolution. Talk to them about the choices you made in the past and why they did (or didn't) work. Evaluate all of your personalized decisions for what you would want them to do in same the situation. Teach your followers that mistakes or failures are always possible, and give them examples from your own life experiences. As we read in Paul's letter to Timothy; "And that from a child thou hast known the holy scriptures, which are able to make thee wise unto salvation through faith which is in Christ Jesus" (2 Timothy 3:15, KJV.) Align your decision to God's Word and teach them God's point of view. Live the life and walk the talk without hypocrisy.

Leaders model responsibility by being accountable. Define the follower's responsibilities and hold them accountable as you assume your own responsibilities. Use your talents well (profitably) and to the glory of God. Teach your followers to be responsible for the talents they have by standing accountable for your own actions. Include your followers in your major decision-making just as Jesus engaged the disciples in feeding the five thousand. Include them in the process so that they will better understand how things work in the ministry.

Leaders model obedience to the law by being law-abiding. Being subject to authority must be modeled to help others cultivate the habit of subordination and respect for the law. Leaders must demonstrate by their actions that they follow the law, even simple laws such as obeying road signs, not cheating on your taxes, and respecting authority. Encourage followers to be law-abiding in all that they do. It is right and a good example; however, to show that you disagree with specific actions that are contrary to Biblical teaching. It is not acceptable, though, as the leader-servant to disrespect the law and people in authority or in a hateful manner toward another person. Such attitudes do not reflect Christ's teaching of respecting people in authority or loving all people. We must be careful to differentiate our hatred of the sins people commit and the people themselves. Expect the best from people, but not perfection. Compliment others for their best efforts, not their perfections. Affirm them when they do well.

Leaders model integrity and self-reliance worthy of emulation. The leader-servant must always be truthful and sincere. Integrity is best taught when the leader walks in integrity, as the following example: "The just man walketh in his integrity: his children are blessed after him" (Proverbs 20:7, KJV) A leader-servant that exudes integrity and self-reliance worthy of emulation must:

- Be a person of his or her word by keeping promises.
- Model Godly principles by being godlike in principles.
- Prepare followers for ministry through hands-on teaching and practicing Godly principles such as faith, forgiveness, diligence, hard work, truthfulness, and belief in God's promises.
- Intentionally show that you take wisdom from the Word of God.
- Lead followers by example to think of the welfare of others and perform acts of generosity.
- Be a giving leader of the time, money, affirmations, and appreciation.

Leaders model credibility as a sacred regard for truth. This can be done by avoiding a lying tongue, which will throw a barrier in the way of holiness. Lying is dictated easily and is one simple way to lose credibility. Every false statement, concealment, exaggeration, and broken promise will only damage the trust of your followers. Be honest with your follower and freely share your wilderness experience, both your failures and successes.

MODELING TEMPERANCE THROUGH SELF-CONTROL

Leader-servants model temperance in followers by controlling their temper. Intemperance in thought, word, or deed is simply an indulgence. Just as God appointed parents to be the immediate guardian of their children's hearts (their happiness, virtue, and hopes), a leader-servant as a shepherd must serve as a guardian to his sheep. Beware how you sow "seeds of intemperance" in your followers. Control your temper. Communicate clearly.

As parents, we love to see our good qualities reflected in our children. At the same time, it pains us when we see them exhibit some of our negative qualities. One of my bad qualities was my temper. My temper and its associated anger did not allow my wife to see how much I loved her. She always wondered how I could love but could not control my anger. My affirmations of love did not match my actions. She also wondered why I never showed my anger to people that report to me that she knew were difficult to work with. I see myself in my first child and daughter—all the good, and yes, the temper, too. I confessed to her that being in control of one's emotions is an important virtue. I love my daughter dearly and admire some of her good qualities, including hard work, ambition, interpersonal skills, selflessness, contagious leadership qualities, and love of God. After receiving an undergraduate degree from Yale, she returned to our home in Pittsburgh to continue her Ph.D. However, her temper had to go. We became a team, working together and sharing ways to deal with this weak point. Now my daughter is married to a wonderful man of God and is serving as a professor in one of the great institutions in the world. I have seen my daughter transform to become more beautiful inside. I have also watched my four children dedicate their lives to living for God. Each one of them followed the example of keeping to the family altar with God in their families. Family rules and values as they were growing up were integrated into the Word of God without ever forcing those values down their throats. They grew up to see those rules as the right path to follow.

SUMMARY 5
DEVELOPING THE ACTS OF EMULATION-MODELING

Before starting this exercise, please read and follow the instruction in the preface of this workbook. Answers to these questions are contained in this chapter. Completion of these exercises after reading the chapter should take 60-90 minutes.

Discovering the Acts of Emulation Modeling

1. Define emulation-modeling
2. How did Jesus show the disciples a pattern to follow in leadership How did he model responsibility?
3. When Paul said, "Be imitators of me as I am of Christ" (1 Corinthians 11:1, ESV) what was he talking about? See Peter teaching in (1 Peter 5:2-3).
4. What does overseeing the flock mean? See Apostle Paul's letters to Timothy (Timothy 1 and 2 and Titus) consisting of what can be referred to as a leadership training manual about discipleship by modeling Chris-tlikeness. Was Paul talking about training skills or training character? (Titus 2; 12).

Practicing Acts of Emulation-Modeling

Emulation- Modeling referred to the act of modeling the way to give followers specific examples or pictures of how to pursue the goal of serving. Fill out the missing information for strategies to model emulation for your followers

1. What are some practical ways leader model emulation (Philippians 4:13).
2. A corporate body survives only if each member of the organization is engaged to do their part. What are some ways an organizational leader must consider:
3. In what specific ways must Leaders model integrity and self-reliance worthy of emulation.

CHAPTER 6
DEVELOPING THE ACTS OF EMULATION-FOLLOWING

Jesus identified behavioral intentions, translated those intentions into actions by initiation, modeled the path they must follow to meet a goal, and finally challenged his followers to perform an action that they otherwise would not perform. In this final process of leading by emulation, Jesus empowered the desired change by challenging his disciples. Leading by example means "doing what I do" rather than "doing what I say" and is a critical element of leading by emulation. *Follow- Emulation* means leading by ensuing what has been learned from credible teachers or leading by using what you have received. Many times in Jesus's teachings and ministry, He charged the disciples to instruct others by following His guidance and values. Furthermore, Jesus at the end of His earthly ministry commissioned the disciples and later sent the Holy Spirit to empower them to spread His gospel. In this case, the disciples continued to follow Jesus through the indwelling Holy Spirit.

Jesus modeled that change is possible and that the disciples must be inside-out leaders. Here are a few other challenges that increase your ability to lead using emulation skills:

FOLLOWING THE EXAMPLE AND LEAVE NO ALTERNATIVE OPTION.

Jesus challenged his followers by showing them why they should follow Him and the benefits of living a blessed life through service. Jesus challenged them by accepting no options and giving no alternatives; he gave a simple command to follow. How can a leader tell his team to be punctual to a meeting when he or she comes in late most of the time for a no-good reason? How can a supervisor expect his staff to be organized, while he loses files entrusted to him? The practice of "do as I say, not as I do" is an easy way to lose the trust and confidence of your staff but also can lead to reduced motivation and accountability. It dampens the followers' willingness to accept challenges, who may feel that if what you say is not good enough for you, then why should they do it? Double standards are part of power control leadership and are the same as having no standards and no sense of responsibility. Such practices destroy the willingness or readiness of followers to accept challenges above their normal duties.

FOLLOWING THE CHRIST-LIKE IMAGE TO EMULATE

According to our leadership-by-example model, leader-servants are to serve by leading through emulation. Show how to lead by serving based on your sacrifice to others and how you overcame challenges. For example, one of the challenges to overcome is a leader's traditional hold on power and control. Demonstrate that you have no problems sharing power with followers. This means leading people by your Christ-like actions that followers see and to which they can relate. Throughout history, the life of Jesus and his teachings have proven to be indisputably authentic. Hence, a leader's Christ-like actions are the standards the follower sees more than any employment manual. The primary responsibility of a leader is to show the followers the way to follow by leading the way. Jesus challenges His disciples to do what was not natural to them by showing them how and why. Demonstrate actions that anyone can choose that will change the present into a better future. A leader serving as an example creates a clear image of the possibilities and provides inspiration to followers to desire to follow. When Jesus stooped low to wash his disciples' feet, I believe they looked at Him and accepted His challenge with no equivocation. In their minds, and ours too, one could see "It is possible! If He can do it, I can follow! I can do it also." His example made it easier for Peter to follow, from wanting nothing, including forgiveness, which hindered his relationship with God, to desiring all of Jesus. Peter moved from one extreme of "no" to the other side unrestrained desiring "all of me," and he grew to be a great leader. Peter wrote; "To this you were called, because Christ suffered for you, leaving you an example, that you should follow in his steps" (1 Peter 2:24, NIV).

CHAPTER 6
DEVELOPING THE ACTS OF EMULATION-FOLLOWING

FOLLOWING YOUR PRIORITIES WITH PASSION

Can you think of someone that you know who defined his leadership by closely emulating someone else? What exactly do we follow to reproduce that person's example as emulators of that person? The success of the Apostle Paul's ministry was that with incredible passion, he followed the example that Jesus set. To Paul, there was no other alternative. The Apostle Paul's examples are defined by his priorities to follow Jesus' example. Your passion communicates what matters most to you to your followers and that those things are worthy to learn and practice.

The starting point is to identify what the priorities are and follow them with passion and the guidance of the Holy Spirit. However, identifying the priorities is not enough. You must focus on an action plan to achieve those priorities. The success you desire from knowing your assets is to emulate Christ-like leadership skills. The first action is to identify and let go of things that do not matter in servant ministry. We see the danger of a crowded life in Solomon. He pursued so many wrong, self-serving goals that he could not identify what he really wanted. As a result, he despaired until the last days of his leadership (Ecclesiastics 12: 13-14). A leader cannot reach a point of focus until he or she can identify an opportunity and what he or she really wants out of the opportunity. The opportunity drives the motivation to focus on maximizing it. This requires focusing on a set of measurable goals, and associated action plans to drive the process and muster the energy to achieve the goals.

The Apostle Paul passionately followed the example of Jesus. Let us identify the priorities of Jesus in His 3-year ministry and examine how Paul followed them. Paul was inspired by Christ's example and attempted to follow His model closely as possible. He clearly demonstrated Jesus' command to serve one another as He served. Paul expressed it this way: "Be ye followers of me even as I also am of Christ" (1 Corinthians 11:1, KJV). Here are a few more examples of Christ's priorities that Paul identified and followed passionately:

He followed Jesus' priority on relationships. Jesus had an intense relationship and focus on God the Father, praising Him, meditating on Him, worshiping Him, listening to Him, and glorifying Him (Mark 1:35), Paul followed His example with passion: he focused on Jesus and ministered to others out of the overflow of the anointing of Jesus through prayer, meditation, praise, reflection, and an empowered vision. Jesus ministered to his disciples and equipped them to reproduce His example to disciple others. With Christ's relationship with the Father and the mission set before him, Paul remained fixed and disciplined to finish the mission.

He followed Jesus' priority on discipleship. Jesus focused his attention on his disciples, explaining things to His disciples more than he did to the multitudes. He also listened to them and answered their questions, rebuked and corrected them whenever necessary, and affirmed and encouraged them (Mark 3:14, 15) Paul followed the same example of building their leadership character and values, teaching, shepherding, healing, evangelizing, and engaging in fellowship. Paul had a disciple-making, coaching, and encouraging relationship with Timothy and Titus, as well as other men he trained.

He followed Jesus' priority on teaching. Jesus taught His disciples exactly what they needed to know about the mission, the message, the mandate, the method, and a life of service to others. He then commissioned them to expand the ministry to all nations. As he was leaving them for heaven, Jesus said to them, "Therefore, go and make disciples of all nations, baptizing them by the name of the Father and of the Son and of the Holy Spirit, and teaching them to obey everything I have commanded you. And surely I am with you always, to the very end of the age" (Matthew 28:19-20, NIV) To continue applying His teaching; Jesus endowed them with the power of the Holy Spirit. In teaching His disciples about faith, on several occasions, Jesus demonstrated faith himself. For example, as they watched Peter walk on water, he taught Peter and the disciples that with faith, they could do the impossible. And, in calming the storm, he taught that the presence of God stills the storm.

He followed Jesus' priority on love Jesus taught and demonstrated love through his ultimate sacrifice and death on the cross. He challenged His disciples to live out the example He showed them, which is to love one another. Paul closely emulated Jesus' passion for the priorities he was working on. Paul's passion and love for the Lord were demonstrated by his complete dedication to his mission, which was patterned after Christ's example. Just as reconciling humanity to God was part of God's plan for Jesus (and was something for which Jesus died), Paul learned from Jesus' examples that love for people was something worth dying for. God's workers must arm themselves with this basic attitude as much as Christ suffered for us in the flesh (1 Peter 4:1)

He followed Jesus' passion for priorities. The Apostle Paul's passion inspired him to give up his personal rights, privileges, and preferences to gain Christ: "But what things were gain to me, these I have counted loss for Christ. Yet indeed I also count all things loss for the excellence of the knowledge of Christ Jesus my Lord, for whom I have suffered the loss of all things, and count them as rubbish…" (Philippians 3:7-10, NKJV)

Paul was focused on finishing strong, running the race, or fighting to win and in the corruptible crown by disciplining the body; his passion can be measured by his mind to suffer for the sake of the work of the gospel. Paul was very passionate about Christ and in making Christ known to others; he was fervent in following the example of Christ that he became all things to all men to win as many to Christ (1 Corinthians 9:19-27, NIV). Here are a few other examples of key principles and priorities to emulate from the life of Jesus. A leader-servant must:

- Serve others and not desire to be ministered to; He must choose to serve as a servant.
- Deny self to please others, not self
- Develop others by adding value to them.
- Accept mistreatment by forgiving wrongs.
- Imitate Christ by looking to Jesus as our model.
- Remain humble and teachable.
- Let Christ's purpose for His life prioritize his own life.
- Model Christ-likeness before you lead others to follow.
- Teach responsibility by sharing responsibility.
- Create credibility by building trust and meeting needs.
- Develop and disciple leaders to become future leaders.

Summary 6
Developing the Acts of Emulation-Following

Before starting this exercise, please read and follow the instruction in the preface of this workbook. Answers to these questions are contained in this chapter. Completion of these exercises after reading the chapter should take 60-90 minutes.

Discovering the Acts of Emulation-Following

1. How did Jesus demonstrate acts of emulation-following
2. What does leading ny example mean in this context? Furthermore, Jesus at the end of His earthly ministry commissioned the disciples empower them to spread His gospel. What was the example of emulation-following in this instance?

Practicing the Acts of Emulation-Following

How did Jesus show His followers why they should follow. The practice of "do as I say, not as I do" is an easy way to lose the trust and confidence of your staff but also can lead to reduced motivation and accountability. What is the impact of such attitude on followers?

1. How does the principle of leadership-by-example model emulation by following
2. The primary responsibility of a leader is to show the followers the way to follow by leading the way. How did Jesus challenges His disciples to do what was not natural to them
3. What was the direct impact on Peter "To this you were called, because Christ suffered for you, leaving you an example, that you should follow in his steps" (1 Peter 2:24, NIV).

Following Your Priorities with Passion

1. Can you think of someone that you know who defined his leadership by closely emulating someone else? What exactly do we follow to reproduce that person's example as emulators of that person?

Chapter 6
Developing the Acts of Emulation-Following

2. The Apostle Paul passionately followed the example of Jesus. Identify the priorities of Jesus in His 3-year ministry and examine how Paul followed them. (1 Corinthians 11:1, KJV;
3. (Mark 1:35; Mark 3:14, 15; Matthew 28:19-20, NIV; 1 Peter 4:1; Philippians 3:7-10, NKJV)
4. **Emulation-Following**: Follow the Example and Leave no Alternative Option; follow the Priorities with Passion; and Build Impact from relationships with others.

Model Emulating	By your act of……
Inspiration	Enthusiasm in leading team others
Selflessness-	
Initiation	
Selfless habits	
Humility	
Responsibility	
Obedience	
Integrity	
Credibility	
Temperance	
Good Following	

5. Take the Leadership generosity attribute audit in Table 3.
6. Based on the questions in Table 3. can you identify each of the acts of emulation leadership attribute? What ones did you score 3 ("sometimes") or less than 3? Review and learn and commit to work to improve

Principle of Acts of Emulation-following

Define the Key principles and priorities to emulate from the life of Jesus. Fill in the backs. A leader-servant must:
    a. _____ others and not desire to be ministered to;
    b. He must _____ to serve as a servant.
    c. _____self to please others, not self
    d. Develop others by _____ value to them.
    e. Accept _____by forgiving wrongs.
    f. Imitate Christ by _____ to Jesus as our model.
    g. Remain _____ and teachable.

h. Model _____ before you lead others to follow.
i. Teach _____ by sharing responsibility.
j. Create _____ by building trust and meeting needs.
k. Develop and _____ leaders to become future leaders.

Table 3. Leadership Emulation Attribute Audit					
Servant leadership emulation attribute is the combined acts of initiating an authentic servant attitude as a model of service worthy of following as an example. Assess the quality of your acts of emulation attribute by inserting an X below the number that best describes your response to each statement.					
Item	Acts of Emulation Attribute Check 1= Always; 2= Frequently; 3= Sometimes; 4= Almost Never; 5= Never	1	2	3	4	5
1	I Imitate and look to Jesus as the authentic model to follow.					
2	My acts of humility inspire others to want to emulate me					
3	I model positive behavior that I want others to follow or desire to emulate					
4	I motivate others to serve by living out the reasons to serve.					
5	I model acts of initiating an authentic servant attitude					
6	My personal examples of good works are worthy of emulation by others					
7	In my acts of modeling the way, I show followers specific patterns to follow					
8	I inspire the followers to follow my example by sharing myself with them					
9	I model credibility through my acts of trustworthiness and believability					
10	I develop others by sharing values and experiences from which they can learn.					
	Add up your rating in each column					
Total Score	Guide and Explanation of Score: Check and understand the areas you need to further develop for improvement	Row 11 Total Score =				
10-17	Great Emulation Leadership; keep it up!				
18-25	Above Average emulation; need to work on 25% of the areas				
26-33	Average but developing; need to work on 50% of the areas				
34-41	Below average affection; need to work on 75% of the areas				
42-50	No emulation leadership ; work on all the areas				

TOPIC INDEX

About This Book, 22
Affective Compassion, 73, 79
authentic, 24, 26
authentic leadership, 37
Authentic Leadership, 45
Authenticity, 43
Comfort, 41
commitment, 19, 25
Comparisons
   with other works, 40
credibility, 48
Discipleship, 84
   definition of, 27
distinguishes
   a leader's act of giving, 29
Emulate, 66, 67, 69, 70, 74, 75, 82, 86, 88
Functional Definitions, 35
Generosity
   definition of, 29
Generosity c, 29
giving, 29
   habit of, 29
humility, 62, 87, 88
Impact, 87
inside-out, 46
Joshua, 19
law of, 42
Leader as Servant Leadership, 42
   definition, 25
Leader First., 23
Leader-as-Servant Leadership, 23

leader-servant's affection-attribute
   definition, 48
leadership, 25
Leadership Attributes, 43
Leadership Inner Value system, 25
Model, 23
Model accountability by
   being responsible, 76
Model Credibility
   regard for truth, 77, 87
Model Integrity
   by self-reliance, 77, 79, 87
Model Obedience
   law abiding, 77, 87
Model Temperance
   by self-control, 78, 87
Moses, 19
Navigation-attribute, 48
Organizational leadership trust, 32
Personal Outward Authenticity, 47
Practicing Servant Leadership
   Emulation, 58
process, 25
relationships, 87
Servant, 23, 24, 57
suffering, 85, 87
test
   for leader-servant authenticity, 46
   of essential elements of personal
      authenticity, 46, 47
The Leadership Influence-attribute, 41

REFERENCES

[1] Greenleaf, R. (1970). *The Servant as Leader,* Indianapolis: The Robert K. Greenleaf Center

[2] Spears, L. (1996). *"Reflections on Robert K. Greenleaf and servant-leadership."* Leadership & Organization Development Journal, 17(7), 33-35

[3] Russell, R.F. (2001). "The role of values in servant leadership." *Leadership & Organization Development Journal,* 22(2), 76-83

[4] Russell, R.F., and Stone, A.G. (2002). "A review of servant leadership attributes: developing a practical model." *Leadership & Organization Development Journal,* 23(3), 145-15

[5] Terry. R. W (1993). *Authentic Leadership: Courage In Action,* San Francisco, CA ,Jossey-Bass

[6] George, B (2003). *Authentic Leadership: Rediscovering the Secrets to Creating Lasting Value.* San Francisco, CA, Jossey-Bass

[7] Shamir, B. & Eilam, G. (2005). "What's your story? Toward a life-story approach to authentic leadership." Leadership Quarterly, 16, 395–418.

[8] Anderson, GL (2009). Advocacy Leadership: Toward a Post-Reform Agenda in Education, Routledge, New York, 41

[9] Yacobi, B.G. *"Elements of Human Authenticity."* http://www.philosophytogo.org/wordpress/?p=1945, Retrieved, July 15, 2012

[10] George, B (2003). *Authentic Leadership: Rediscovering the Secrets to Creating Lasting Value,* San Francisco, CA, Jossey-Bass

[11] Wosu, SN (2014), *Leader as Servant Leadership Model,* Xulon Press

[18] Bass,B. M. (1985). *Leadership and Performance.* N. Y,: Free Press

[19] Bass, B. M. & Riggio, R. E. (2008). *Transformational Leadership.* Mahwah, New Jersey: Lawrence Erlbaum Associates, Inc.

[20] Riggio, Ronald E (2009, March 24). "Are You a Transformational Leader?". *Psychology Today.* Found online at http://blogs.psychologytoday. com/blog/cutting-edge-leadership/200903/are-you-transformational-leader

www.ingramcontent.com/pod-product-compliance
Lightning Source LLC
LaVergne TN
LVHW061558070526
838199LV00077B/7099